"If one loves, one will do anything."

Rennie's voice broke and she looked away, hoping to avoid Dev Devereaux's discerning gaze.

But Dev smiled mockingly. "I wonder about you, Rennie Baxter. You're remote, delicate, dreamy. But you'll drop down from the sky on the end of a parachute, watch a man fight a scrub bull and stand in the middle of a cattle stampede, all with never a thought of danger. And now—am I wrong, or are you insinuating that you'd live with a man like Jake Ridley—a man who already has a wife?"

Rennie hesitated, then nodded defiantly. It wasn't true, and she didn't really care about Jake. But she couldn't let Dev suspect that it was he whom she loved!

OTHER
Harlequin Romances
by DOROTHY CORK

1511—WHERE BLACK SWANS FLY
1549—A NIGHT FOR POSSUMS
1644—WAYAWAY
1668—SUMMER MOUNTAIN
1692—BUTTERFLY MONTANE
1714—SPIRIT OF THE SUN
1757—THE GIRL AT SALTBUSH FLAT
1784—THE RED PLAINS OF JOUNIMA
1812—A PROMISE TO KEEP
1876—GATE OF THE GOLDEN GAZELLE
1894—QUICKSILVER SUMMER
1927—WANDALILLI PRINCESS
1966—RED DIAMOND
2057—DREAM TIME AT BIG SKY
2115—BREAKERS ON THE BEACH
2199—A THOUSAND MILES AWAY

Many of these titles are available at your local bookseller
or through the Harlequin Reader Service.

For a free catalogue listing all available Harlequin Romances,
send your name and address to:

HARLEQUIN READER SERVICE,
M.P.O. Box 707, Niagara Falls, N.Y. 14302
Canadian address: Stratford, Ontario, Canada N5A 6W2

or use coupon at back of book.

Heart of the Whirlwind

by

DOROTHY CORK

Harlequin Books

TORONTO • LONDON • NEW YORK • AMSTERDAM
SYDNEY • HAMBURG • PARIS

Original hardcover edition published in 1974
by Mills & Boon Limited

ISBN 0-373-02253-0

Harlequin edition published April 1979

CHAPTER ONE

RENNIE STOWED the neatly repacked picnic basket away in the trunk of the car, closed the lid down, turned around, and stood perfectly still, a small smile tilting the corners of her rather wide mouth. Down in the shade of the river gums, Dr. Grace Warren, who had been driving all day, was relaxing for half an hour, and Nancy had fallen asleep, too, on the edge of the cotton rug.

Only Rennie remained awake.

Everything around her had an air of unreality. Even the very fact that she was here. The Outback shimmered in the burning heat of late afternoon. It waited, it listened; it was near but strangely remote. Unimaginably dramatic colors sang all around her—the bright orange red of the earth softened by clumps of gray green trees or a scattering of blue bushes, the clear brilliant green of the water hole by which they had picnicked, the sizzling scarlet of a dragonfly that, as she watched, darted and hung, darted and hung hypnotically across the water's surface, the one moving thing within sight.

Rennie pushed back her bright brown hair and her eyes dreamed. She was here in the Outback—she really was. And on her way to what adventure? She was curiously certain that there was far more awaiting her than simply the job of cook on Silver Springs cattle station. That, at any rate, was only a temporary job—it would last only while Dr. Grace and Nancy were visiting. And when they returned to Adelaide, she didn't have the slightest idea whether she would return with them. It was certainly not with a city job in mind that she had left England and come to Australia, but she had taken on the job of home help in the Warren household while waiting for something else to turn up. They had said at the agency that they couldn't find her anything in the country immediately but since she could cook, she might meanwhile take the Adelaide Hills position.

It was only later that Rennie suspected they were anxious to please Dr. Grace rather than Rennie Baxter. At the time she suspected that their reluctance to send her to the Outback was because her looks belied her inclinations. She was a tall, slender girl of twenty-two, with a wide mouth, sea-blue eyes and thick brown hair that reached to her shoulders and hung in a heavy fringe across her forehead. There was a small, new scar high on her right cheekbone—the one flaw in a delicate rose-petal skin, though she was more of an outdoor girl than an English rose, as any one of her three older sisters, all of them married, would have admitted. And in fact, she had worried them sick at odd times—ever since their parents had died leaving them feeling responsible for her when she would have preferred to be responsible for herself.

Not that she had proved herself so adept at managing her personal life to date. On the contrary. She had made a bad start in taking up secretarial work and then discovering it did not appeal to her in the least. A winter spent as an *au pair* girl with a French family on the Côte d'Azur when she was nineteen, had brought out an unexpected latent talent: she could cook like an angel. But not in France. Her first love affair and its disastrous ending brought her back to England in a rush. And there she drifted from one job to another in private homes. But she didn't have a diploma, and besides, cooking as a full-time career did not appeal to her. So she had to work for women who expected other things of her—help with the children, the housework and so on. And she was back in her old state of dissatisfaction. She just knew there was more in life if only she could find it—some special niche for Rennald Baxter, who so badly wanted to embrace life with open arms.

She was staying with her sister Anita in the north of England when she thought she had found it. A chance Saturday afternoon spent at a weekend parachuting club, and Rennie was hooked. She took up sky-jumping, and Anita, Margo and Valerie and their respective husbands nearly went out of their minds.

"Do you want to kill yourself?"

She didn't know how many times she heard that accusing question. Of course she didn't want to kill herself, and she tried to explain that as long as you were sensible, parachuting was no more dangerous than any other sport. She had a wonderful instructor, Pete Morgan, and he would never let her do anything until she was ready for it. They simply must trust her.

They didn't.

Nevertheless she returned to secretarial work to pay for her sport and she was really happy. Life was wonderful and exciting and apart from the thrill of the progress she was making as she went from static line jumps to the manually-operated parachute and on to free-falling, she had fallen in love with Pete.

And then, completely out of the blue, the whole thing fell apart. Pete produced a fiancée, and Rennie discovered that without him, parachuting had no meaning. She made her last jump, fouling it up for a reason so way-out that no one would have believed it if she had told them about it. She landed in a tree, and the small star-shaped scar on her cheek was her sole memento.

Her sisters actually said, "We told you so," and Rennie didn't let them know she had suffered a hurt far deeper than the cut on her cheek. That Pete could have deceived her as he had when she had believed in him so utterly! If that was what men were like, then she wanted no more of them.

And so, with the throat of her love affair cut, with parachute jumping out, she was desperate to find something new and dramatic to fill her life. It was hearing some women in the bus discussing a TV documentary on Australia that had sent her Down Under. She decided to turn her back on love and all that was familiar and to seek adventure in the mysterious Outback. It was a challenge and it appealed to all that was daring in her.

And now here she was. "My cook," as Dr. Grace had been calling her for just over a month—"in the mulga," as Nancy Warren had put it. And though there were certain men she was going to encounter in the mulga— Tim Lang, Dev Deveraux, Dr. Grace's nephew who was "living in the rough" and even, possibly, that tough wild stockman, Jake Ridley—Rennie was going to keep herself well and truly uninvolved with them.

Except that she really would like to give Jake Ridley a piece of her mind, or at the very least deal out to him a little of the treatment he had handed to Nancy Warren. . . .

She glanced at her watch. She had promised to wake Dr. Grace when the half hour was up, for they still had a long way to go. There were just ten minutes left—time for a stroll by the side of the green water.

But it was so hot that Rennie abandoned her stroll as soon as she reached the red sandy banks. She sat down on the ground, her legs in their light cotton pants stretched out in front of her. Her mind was too active for sleep, and her thoughts returned to yesterday when Dr. Grace, coming home with Nancy after a day in the city, had opened the letter that had sent them off on this journey across the Flinders Ranges.

Rennie had come from the kitchen where she was cooking *poulet cocotte grand'mère* to join the others in a predinner drink when she found Dr. Grace, large and overwhelming, frowning over her letter. Nancy, who was nineteen and fetching, though a trifle overweight, was trying on a flimsy see-through hat of pale blue straw at the mirror, the sofa behind her littered with wrappings from all the slightly crazy new gear she had bought during the day's shopping spree. Nancy was spoiled, and could have been unbearable. But for some reason Rennie found her extremely likable especially with that kind of primitive naturalness about her.

"Help yourself to a drink, Rennald," Dr. Grace said absently, eyes narrowed, brow furrowed over her letter.

Rennie, already sensing a crisis of some kind, did so.

Nancy asked, "Do you like my hat?"

But before Rennie could reply, Dr. Grace exclaimed emphatically, "I'm simply not going to put up with this nonsense of Dev's any longer! It's absurd for him to persist in living out in that godforsaken desert at Nimmitibel." She reached for her glass on the small table nearby and downed its contents quickly.

Nancy pulled off her hat and sat on the arm of a chair.

"What's happened now, mother? I thought you said you'd give Dev six months after granddaddy died, and then he'd be back at Silver Springs like a shot. When we got back from New Zealand—just before we got Rennie— you were sure of it." She grimaced at Rennie. "Family troubles. Mother thinks my cousin Dev should live and marry and procreate at Silver Springs, the old family home, though she thinks it's deadly herself."

Her mother ignored this gibe. "Dev is proposing

virtually to hand over the property to this boy of Meg Lang's, who can't be more than twenty-three or four. Fortunately, since we're now coowners, he needs my agreement before he appoints a permanent manager, and I'm certainly not going to sign on some lad who's still feeling his way, even though he is Stan Lang's son. No, I could understand Dev clearing out during father's lifetime. They could never have coexisted, they were both unbearably strong willed and pigheaded, and as long as he could stand upright the old man would never have surrendered an ounce of his authority. But now Dev really should go home. He owes it to the family to live at Silver Springs.''

Rennie listened, trying to piece it all together and never for a moment dreaming that she would be heading for Silver Springs herself the very next day.

"What about Nimmitibel?'' demanded Nancy.

"Dev could leave Nimmitibel to be managed by that head stockman of his—what's his name—Ridley.''

Nancy sat up straight.

"Jake Ridley! How I hate that man! He's so handsome you wouldn't believe it, but I've never met anyone more horrid. Or more inhuman.'' She turned to Rennie, her face animated. "Look, Rennie—a girl friend and I went to the Outback for the school holidays one year. We drove over to Nimmitibel with one of grandaddy's station hands, and I asked this Jake Ridley type if we could go out to the muster camp. Talk about bush hospitality! He didn't want any 'females' hanging around the camp. Imagine it—females! In his opinion all females are brainless and scheming. We didn't want to see the muster camp, we just wanted to flirt with the stockmen—or so Jake said. He's about the only person I've ever hated in my life. Libbie and I were just innocent little schoolgirls and we could have sunk through the ground. Don't you think it was rotten to talk to little kids that way?"

"You were fifteen, if I remember rightly," said her mother dryly, "and very well developed. . . . However, Ridley *is* a tough unsociable character, and that's why it would be so simple for Dev to let him manage Nimmitibel. . . . How's dinner, Rennie?"

"Ready the minute you want it," said Rennie, getting up at once. She had been more than a little fascinated by the conversation. She had not known before that the Warrens were connected with country life in any way, and she wondered exactly where Nimmitibel was, but did not like to ask. She went out to the kitchen a little reluctant to miss the rest of the discussion.

"So anyhow," said Nancy, not ten minutes later as they all sat down to dinner, "what do you propose to do about Dev, mother?"

"We'll drive to Silver Springs tomorrow," said Dr. Grace. "I'll make a thorough check on what's happening there. I'll look at the stock and the bores and the feed and see exactly what's being neglected or mismanaged."

"How will you know, mother?" Nancy wondered. "I wouldn't have a clue."

"I was brought up in the bush," said Dr. Grace. "In any case, I'm quite sure Silver Springs needs taking in hand. Extraordinary old character though father was, he couldn't possibly have efficiently managed a property that size during the last few years of his life. There must be a lot to do to put things right."

"And Tim Lang is too young, but Dev is just right. . . . How long will we stay?"

"Since I'll simply refuse to sign on young Lang, we'll stay until Dev agrees to go back where he belongs. He's stubborn, but my mind is made up. I don't care how long it takes."

Rennie listened and wondered. She didn't suppose she fitted anywhere in this. She would probably have to look for another job. Rather thoughtfully, she got on with her meal. She would be told what was to happen in good time.

She was told over coffee.

"You will come with us, Rennald. If we are to eat decent meals, I must take my own cook. I remember the food we ate at Silver Springs when I was a child—and I simply refuse to live on damper and beef. I'm long past the stage where I can tolerate that kind of thing."

Rennie felt her spirits lift with excitement. So she was to be cook on an Outback station! It was exactly the kind of thing she had come to Australia for! And they were to start the very next day. Dr. Grace certainly didn't believe in wasting time.

It proved to be a long and grueling drive, and much farther than Rennie, who had tried to find the approximate locality of Silver Springs on her map, had anticipated. But Dr. Grace, who was large and healthy and had a will that Rennie suspected was quite as strong as her father's or her nephew's, took it all in her stride. One would have thought she knew the road backward, she was so completely imperturbable. Through the ever-increasing heat of the day she drove relentlessly on, bumping over rough corrugated tracks, ploughing through sand drifts, skidding across sticky yellow clay-pans. Even when the road looked as if it were leading nowhere at all, even when it seemed to disappear altogether as it quite frequently did on the endless stretches of saltbush plain, she was undeterred.

Rennie had complete faith in her. It was Nancy who asked half humorously, "Are you quite sure you know where you're going, Mother? I would hate to be stranded in the middle of the Outback and die of thirst. I'm too young to accept it philosophically. Aren't you, Rennie?''

Nancy, thought Rennie, was quite a character. And at that point in her reflections, she became aware that Nancy at least was awake again and coming down to join her.

The green water was suddenly crisscrossed by red and blue and green dragonflies, and a flock of corellas appeared and settled in the river gums. The sky that all day had been a pale, pure pulsing blue, began to turn green, and a little of the heat left the air. Within five minutes they were on their way again.

As they bumped and bounced determinedly over the track, Nancy asked in her down-to-earth way, "What if the Langs don't want us at Silver Springs now that granddaddy isn't there any longer? What shall we do, mother? I just hate being *de trop.*''

"My dear child—" Dr. Grace lit a cigarillo and managed somehow to steer the dust-coated car deftly enough to narrowly avoid an enormous pothole "—I am part owner of Silver Springs. I am employing the Langs— however much against my will—and they will simply have to put up with us whether they like it or not . . . though as a rule Outback people are glad to have company of any kind. However, if it will make you feel any better, we'll probably have to spend some of our time at Nimmitibel. As far as I'm concerned, it will be sheer martyrdom. Bill would turn over in his grave if he knew that his son was living there.''

Rennie, who had actually as well as metaphorically taken a backseat all day, for the first time felt a tremor of doubt. How would Mrs. Lang like the idea of her coming along to do the cooking? Rennie hoped she would not be too put out. She disliked treading on people's toes.

Silence fell, the clear green light of evening began to

fade, a shaft of fiery color flared across the sky, and in no time at all it was dark.

It seemed a long, long time later when they reached a wide gate in a side track leading from the bumpy road. Nancy hopped out nimbly and opened it, and when they drove through they were on the Silver Springs cattle station. The silhouette of a long, flat-topped hill lay against the horizon, and Rennie saw the shadows of cattle in the shelter of trees as they drove swiftly along. Away ahead, yellow lights glowed. Minutes later, and two gates later, they had reached the homestead.

Rennie was so tired as she stumbled from the car onto a graveled square outside the garden fence that all she wanted was to sleep. She scarcely took in the two people who greeted them as they entered the garden—Meg Lang, a plump middle-aged woman, her son Tim, a stocky broad-shouldered young man. It was all vague as a dream. The garden smelled sweetly musky in the warm night, and when she entered the house after crossing a wide veranda, she was vaguely aware of comfort and a slightly faded elegance, somehow unexpected out here in the middle of nowhere. Gilt-framed oil paintings hung in the big entrance hall, there was a soft carpet and a couple of cedar chairs with satin brocade coverings. Then a long passageway with a lot of doors opening off it, and somehow Rennie was in a bedroom by herself—a bedroom equipped with the most inviting-looking bed and a shining bathroom through a curtained doorway. She showered and fell into the bed, barely bothering to pull the cool linen sheet over herself. Someone brought her a tray with tea and thin sandwiches, but she was asleep before she could touch any of it.

THE NEXT DAY was completely and utterly different in every way from anything she had even vaguely imagined.

To begin with, she slept late although she had meant to be up at seven—the hour at which she usually rose in Adelaide. She was awakened by Nancy's robust voice close to her ear.

"Wake up, Rennie, or you'll miss out on the picnic races!"

Rennie sat up with an effort and pushed the hair away from her face, blinking the sleep away from her sea-blue eyes. The air was already hot, and the day had well and truly begun. She should have been up to get the breakfast long ago! As for picnic races—she was here to do the cooking.

Dressed in brief white shorts and sleeveless shirt, Nancy drawled out, "Now don't get into a panic. Mother's been fed. She ate a hugh plateful of steak and eggs and she didn't utter a word of complaint. The house girls have done the washing up and everything's under control. Tim's gone out on the range, but he'll be back soon. He's a bright lad and he knows we're here to bury Caesar not to praise him, even though Mother didn't reveal her deadly mission last night. She played it very cool, and Tim played it even cooler. I wish you'd been there to listen instead of collapsing into bed."

Rennie, listening and amused as she often was by Nancy, padded over to the dressing table, gave her hair a few vigorous brush strokes, and said mildly, "I'm glad you woke me. But of course I won't come to the picnic races. I'm the cook."

"There's no one to cook for today," said Nancy positively. "We've got a picnic basket packed, and Meg's made scones, and we're about to have morning tea on the side veranda. If you hurry, you can eat enough to make up for missing breakfast before Tim turns up. So get a move on.''

She sauntered off, and Rennie somewhat uncertainly made for the shower. Suddenly she felt nervous. She didn't know whether the cook ought to go to the picnic races. She didn't know how she would be received. And she felt a little bit afraid of meeting the Outback people. Maybe they would ask her all the questions she dreaded—personal questions that Dr. Grace had never thought of asking.

When she had showered she dressed quickly in a sleeveless cotton dress and white sandals. Then she leaned close to her reflection in the wall mirror that had a polished cedar frame, and with makeup camouflaged her scar. She was peculiarly sensitive about that scar—it was a symbol of love betrayed.

When she went out, Dr. Grace and Meg Lang were on the shady side veranda, and beyond the garden, the saltbush plain stretched out to the flat horizon. Rennie's apologies for her late appearance were passed over carelessly by Dr. Grace and she was helped lavishly to tea and scones by Meg. Then Dr. Grace, long legs crossed, manner blunt and uncompromising, proceeded to ignore her and to tell their hostess, ''I'm going to be quite frank with you, Meg. I'm not at all in favor of appointing Tim as manager of Silver Springs. Besides the indisputable fact that he's far too young and inexperienced, I feel very strongly that my nephew should be here. And I intend to see him here before I leave.''

She paused, and the other woman said with a good-humored firmness, ''You'll have a hard job to shift Dev, Dr. Grace. He hasn't lived here since he left school and he hasn't wanted to. He's made Nimmitibel his home and his love, and he's happy there.''

Dr. Grace's large face flushed with annoyance.

"That's all very well, but he should marry and have a family. And what woman is willing to marry a man who's living on the edge of the desert in conditions that are barely civilized? Would you, Rennald?"

The sudden question disconcerted Rennie, who felt herself color painfully. At this moment in time, she was not in the least interested in marrying any man. As for Dev Deveraux, she didn't know a single thing about him except that he was stubborn and that he was living out in the rough. She looked at her employer helplessly, but of course the question was purely rhetorical. Dr. Grace wasn't really interested in her opinion.

"Now here," Dr. Grace swept on, "a girl could be happy if she liked the Outback. Nimmitibel in comparison has simply nothing to offer—it's a godforsaken bit of country, as dry as dust and completely cut off from the world the moment there's a decent fall of rain, which heaven knows is seldom enough. Dev should leave it in the hands of that head stockman of his. He apparently prefers to live out at the muster camps rather than sleep under a roof, in any event." She broke off and glanced toward the house. "It breaks my heart to see this lovely old homestead virtually abandoned by the family."

The other woman looked amused in a kindly way. She was very different from Dr. Grace. Her plump face still bore traces of prettiness, and her blue eyes were honest and guileless. She said placidly, "Well, I wouldn't call it abandoned. I love the old place and I look after it. It's been the only home I've known since Stan and I married and he brought me here when Mr. Deveraux made him head stockman." She shifted and moved an ashtray so that it was within reach of Dr. Grace, who was spilling ashes on the polished floorboards. "When Tim marries, I'm sure it will be home to him, even though he doesn't own the property. He always used to love coming back here for school holidays and riding with his father to the muster. It was partly for his sake that I stayed on after Stan died, though I'd been keeping house and doing the cooking so long that the boss—your father," she corrected herself, "would have been lost if I'd gone. I'm not saying Tim knows the business nearly as well as Dev, but he's a good boy and he's learning. And he's not too proud to ask for advice. I really don't think you need worry if Dev decides to put Tim permanently in charge here, Dr. Grace. His heart is here, just as Dev's is at Nimmitibel."

"Oh, for goodness' sake," said Dr. Grace, plainly annoyed. "Let's not be sentimental. Hearts haven't anything to do with business, and you're forgetting that I have as much say as Dev when it comes to who's to be in charge here. Dev exiled himself when he was young and intolerant about a homestead that was never built as a family home. Justice must be done."

"All the same, Nimmitibel's not such a bad old homestead," said the other woman. "It could be made quite comfortable." She smiled at Rennie who had been sitting listening in silence and, more as a game than anything else, trying to decide whose side she was on. At the moment, she was inclined to be on Meg Lang's side, which, seeing that she was employed by Dr. Grace, was not very diplomatic of her. However, quite certainly no one was going to ask her opinion, so it didn't really matter all that much. Meg poured her another cup of tea and continued. "As for Dev's marrying—well, I was going to give you the news, Dr. Grace. He's expecting houseguests in a day or so—Isobel Sandison and her aunt. Isobel came here on holiday not long ago with Lynette, my second eldest daughter, you might remember. I suspected at the time that she and Dev were attracted to each other and now he's invited her to Nimmitibel."

Dr. Grace's eyes had narrowed. She leaned back and surveyed her cigarillo with a look of satisfaction. "Then if Dev has marriage in mind, it's a point on my side. No woman would live at Nimmitibel if she knew she could live here instead. And she shouldn't be asked to."

"If she loves him, she'll live wherever he asks her," said Meg simply, and Rennie mentally added a "hear, hear" to that.

"Sentimental rubbish," said Dr. Grace briskly. She rose majestically. "I'll drive around today and see what's happened on the property since father died."

"Oh, that will keep! You must come to the picnics."

"I will certainly not go to the picnics," said Dr. Grace decidedly. "I abhor picnic races. Heat and dust and a lot of clowning around and drunkenness."

"The men from Nimmitibel will be there. You'll want to see Dev."

"Not under those circumstances. Besides, I'm not ready to talk to Dev yet. I'll go over to Nimmitibel and see my nephew and his houseguests when I know a little more about what's going on here."

Rennie exhaled her breath gently. That settled her little problem, then. If Dr. Grace was not going to the picnics, then she could not go. She reached forward and took another scone, and frowned when Meg Lang said firmly, "Rennie must come. Visitors always like to go to the picnics and meet everyone."

"It's quite all right, thank you," began Rennie, but Dr. Grace said irritably, "Oh, for God's sake, go, Rennald. I had such an enormous breakfast this morning I'll have indigestion as it is. I won't want to eat another thing all day and I certainly won't need you."

So be it, thought Rennie. The cook had her orders and it was not her place to protest.

All the same, when Dr. Grace had marched determinedly off, she did utter a protest.

"I don't really think I should go to the picnic races, Mrs. Lang. I came here to do the cooking."

Meg Lang laughed. "Don't worry about that, my dear. I've been cooking at Silver Springs for twenty-five years and nobody's complained yet. Dr. Grace won't have indigestion. Still," she added kindly, "it might be nice to get together some time and exchange recipes, and you're welcome to join me in the kitchen and help anytime you like."

"Thank you," said Rennie automatically, and inwardly grimaced. A job should be a job, in her view, and now she felt like a fraud.

"I suppose you have one of those diplomas," said Meg Lang. "I'm just a good plain cook, self-taught at that."

Rennie forced a smile. It would be churlish not to be friendly. "I'm self-taught, too. And I have self-educated taste buds or something, so I can always tell exactly what's in any dish I eat—all the herbs and flavorings and seasonings -everything. And then it's fun to try to reproduce the dish myself."

"I'll have to put you to the test! But now if I were you I'd run along and take off those stockings and find a hat. It'll be hot at the picnics."

Rennie did as she was told.

THEY DROVE about sixty miles to the picnics, which were being held at Utmaowie, a neighboring property. The red sun poured down its heat onto the plains. On a wide shimmering flat beside a dried-up riverbed where only a few pools of water provided meeting places for birds, and mirrors for the rough red desert mulgas leaning down to their strange primitive reflections, people from the Outback were gathered to race their horses and to exchange news and gossip. Rennie had decided to go carefully until she got the feel of the people and the feel of the country. With Tim Lang—her first Outback man, as it were—it was easy enough. Tim was nice-looking and very young, and his mother obviously doted on him, though she was a little anxious about the cool impersonality of his politeness to the visitors. As Nancy had implied, it looked as though he very much suspected that Dr. Grace's mission was not a friendly one. He was wary.

That suited Rennie very well, for she was wary herself. But it irked Nancy, who would not leave him alone. She sat next to him in the car, she made comments, she asked questions, she teased him. She had chosen to wear her new frivolous blue straw hat and she had pinned a bunch of bright artificial cherries to the brim. She also wore a highly unsuitable long blue cotton dress that gave her the air of a Victorian maiden. And gloves. With a crowd of teenagers in the city she might not have looked remarkable, but on an improvised race course in the middle of the Outback she drew every eye. Tim tried hard to be indifferent, to keep his eyes off her, but he didn't succeed, and Rennie was amused at the determined way she hung on his arm pretending to be unaware of his reluctance to have anything to do with her.

To Rennie, it all seemed very young and very naïve and she wondered whether they would end the day friends or enemies. For a while she stayed with Meg, who was enjoying herself immensely with her friends and who introduced Rennie to everyone simply as a visitor to Silver Springs. But presently she wandered off on her own. She didn't really want to stay with the older women, neither did she want to inflict herself on Tim and Nancy. She left the refreshment tents under the gum trees and walked slowly along toward the race track. There were dozens of cars parked in little patches of shade and groups of people talking hard everywhere. There were a few genial bookies, crowds of rowdy stockmen out for a day's enjoyment, a scattering of younger women and girls and a general atmosphere of good fellowship, despite the dust and the heat.

Rennie found her way to the rails and stood there watching the horses and jockeys, feeling just a little bit out of it, a little bit lonely. But presently, as a race began and the horses tore along the track, she forgot herself. Her eye took pleasure in the gleaming horseflesh, the swiftness of the race, the shadows flying, the red dust, the background of low mulga and tall eucalyptus. Around her were excited cries of advice and encouragement to favored jockeys and even to their mounts, and then Nancy came past to nudge her and say in a low voice, "There's that handsome horrid Jake Ridley over near the bookies' stand. I'm going to cut him dead, if I get half a chance."

She moved on and Rennie turned cautiously, looking back over her shoulder from where she was leaning on the rail. She saw a tall, lean-cheeked man, very bronzed, very striking. But not, she thought, instantly critical, as handsome as Nancy made out. Not all *that* handsome. He was talking to a man whose back was toward Rennie, and he stood with a markedly easy grace. He was a big man with broad shoulders. Big, but not heavy, and very, very stylishly proportioned. He wore narrow-legged cotton trousers and a cream shirt with the sleeves rolled up to reveal darkly tanned, muscular forearms. His face was tanned to almost the exact color of his hair. It was a slightly long face, with dark peaking eyebrows and a chin that looked as strong and stubborn as a male chin had any possible right to look.

She summed him up as a very male animal who was decidedly on his own territory. Just possibly, she caught herself conceding, the kind of man you could depend on utterly if you were parachuting. Only, of course, from what Nancy had said, a man like Jake Ridley would not grant a "female" the right to parachute at all. . . .

He turned a little and she thought he was looking at her, but she was not sure. His eyes were slightly screwed up from staring into the glare, no doubt, as stockmen frequently did. Rennie stared back, aware of an odd tingling up and down her spine. *Come and try me out*, she thought. *Come and hand out patronizing remarks to me and I promise I'll match you blow for blow. I'm no helpless schoolgirl—and what's more, I just happen to have as low an opinion of men as you have of women, and I don't mind letting you know it. Come and give me an opening*, she dared him silently. *Nancy Warren will be revenged well and truly!*

Oddly, it was at that exact point in her thoughts that he began to move toward her. Slightly alarmed, Rennie turned back to the racetrack. Of course he had not read her thoughts. Of course he was not coming to challenge her. Jake Ridley would leave women alone.

But a second later, a slightly drawling voice spoke carelessly at her shoulder. "Hello! Didn't I see you arriving with the Silver Springs lot?" She blinked in surprise. It was a beautifully modulated voice, Australian but far from aggressively so. Not really the sort of voice she would have expected from a tough stockman, however handsome he might be. It threw her a little and she turned too quickly, to find herself staring into eyes so dazzlingly blue that they hurt.

She took a tight hold on herself, gave him a cool smile, saying flatly, "That's right. I'm the cook." She thought, *Now try to call me useless!* It gave her an odd pleasure to witness the effect of her statement on him.

He did a kind of double take. There was a flicker of

pure astonishment in the blue eyes, a raising of diabolical eyebrows; their darkness was touched with gold as were his stunningly thick lashes. Then the corners of his slightly crooked mouth curled up and she caught a glimpse of beautiful white teeth.

"The *cook*?" he repeated.

"Why not?" said Rennie. And she discovered that for a man who despised women, this stockman had a most unnerving way of looking at them. At her, at any rate. And she wondered fleetingly just why he had bothered to come and speak to her   if perhaps he made a practice of introducing himself to any female newcomer so that he could then have the pleasure of expounding his views on the female sex in general? *I couldn't care less what you think of me, if you only knew,* she said silently, and her sea-blue eyes stared challengingly at him.

"Well, I wasn't aware that a cook was needed on Silver Springs," he remarked. He leaned against the rail beside her and his arm brushed accidentally against her own mahogany brown against smooth, barely sun-touched feminine skin. His glance went briefly to the racecourse. There was no race in progress at the moment, but something was going on. Various jockeys were riding their mounts down the field, and when one of the horses was jostled, it threw back its head, snorted and reared up, causing a few feminine squeals farther along the rails. He turned back to Rennie.

"Who hired you? And don't tell me a flimsy girl like you arrived on the mail truck."

"Nobody hired me," said Rennie, still cool and offhand. "I just happen to work for Dr. Warren. I came out from Adelaide in her car. Not," she added very distinctly, "that it's any of your business or need concern you in the slightest degree. I don't have it in mind to get mixed up with you or any of the Nimmitibel stockmen in any way at all. Men, being what they are, don't fascinate me all that much, believe me. It's the country I'm interested in, not the male population. And least of all you," she flung out for good measure and was instantly more than a little appalled at her own rudeness.

She saw his jaw harden. She had disconcerted him, and that was great. She added a rider. "I will gladly leave you," she told him, "to the useless, brainless girl whom, sure as fate, it will be your lot to marry. The punishment so often fits the crime."

"Well, well," he said thoughtfully. "That's quite a load you've got off your mind. It would be enlightening to know what's at the back of that more-than-warped attitude of yours, though I hardly dare hope you'll tell me right now. Just possibly we might get around to it later on. In the meantime, we must certainly see that you get a good look around the country you're so interested in."

Rennie bit her lip. "Don't let it bother you." She couldn't think of another thing to say, and on the whole she didn't feel she was making a particularly good job of routing the insufferable Jake Ridley. She was making herself somewhat insufferable, true enough, and she was by now right off balance. It was something to do with the narrow, glinting way he was looking at her. To use a parachuting term, she was definitely unstable. In fact, she felt as if she were floundering head down as she had done on one terrifying occasion early in her parachuting career when her canopy had failed to deploy for an extra second and a half—quite a considerable time when you are about two and a half thousand feet above the ground and on your own.

He was watching her in an oddly speculative way and his gaze had settled, she was quiveringly aware, on the scar on her cheek she had been at some pains to camouflage. She had the strange feeling that he was connecting it in some way with her "warped attitude," and if he was, then of course he was uncannily right. He nodded down at it casually.

"How did that happen? Looks as though the world was not always kind to you."

"What?" asked Rennie, trying to parry the question. She began to wish she hadn't stalled as the tip of a hard brown finger touched her cheekbone lightly yet fierily.

"I got mixed up with a tree," she said, lightly casual. "Nothing exciting." She knew she had flushed and she could feel her cheek burning as it had when the broken branch had torn at her flesh. That scar was a reminder of her last jump, a bitter reminder of Pete and of the faithlessness of men; and despite the fact that she no longer cried at night over Pete, it was still a reminder not to lose her heart to a man unless she made a thorough investigation of him first. And if love had to wait for a thorough investigation of its object, she rather thought its fires would go out. Love that was real was too impatient. And that was one good reason she was not going to fall in love again for a very long time—if ever.

"So you got mixed up with a tree," he repeated, "and it wasn't exciting. Do you know, I don't believe you. I get the feeling that scar of yours is pretty important. I'll tell you something—I spent a great deal of my early childhood among the aboriginals. A lot of the time I was cared for by lubras, since my own mother had died. And they passed on to me something of their intuitive faculties the ESP, if you'd rather put it that way, of their ancient race."

His eyes burned into hers, and despite herself she was intrigued and aware of it and of the weakness of it, and she sought for some way to tell him she couldn't care less about his childhood. But before she could utter a word, he had given a low disturbing laugh and told her, "You are an intriguing and fascinating girl with your searing remarks and your daredevil eyes. You can be sure we'll be seeing more of each other. . . . If you'll excuse me now, I rather think from the shouts that are going on around us that my horse has come in first in the race you've beguiled me into missing—and I must go and slap my jockey on the back. What's your name, by the way?"

"Rennald Baxter. But don't bother making a note of it. No matter what your ESP tells you, I assure you we won't be having anything more to do with each other. For one thing, I'll be far too busy, and for another—"

"For another, you don't like me. Well, that's obvious. But I don't think you're going to be very busy in the Silver Springs kitchen. Meg Lang does all the cooking that's necessary. In fact, there'd be far more sense in your coming to Nimmitibel to cook. And *that* we will talk about presently."

He had taken two steps away and Rennie knew then that somewhere along the line she had made a miscalculation. Her error was confirmed when he turned back and said, "I'm Dev Deveraux, by the way. But I presume you know that."

He smiled and left, and Rennie stared after him white-lipped and completely speechless.

CHAPTER TWO

SHE WAS APPALLED at the mad, meaningless things she had said to Dr. Grace's nephew. She knew she would have to apologize, to explain somehow, without passing on Nancy's opinion of Jake Ridley. But it was not going to be easy, and she didn't suppose that Dev Deveraux would be terribly pleased to have been mistaken for his own head stockman.

What exactly did I say to him? she wondered on and off all through the rest of that hot dusty day. She had, in a way, lost her head. She had forgotten that she was avenging Nancy—he had had such an unsettling effect on her—and she had tossed in some very rude remarks and insinuations completely on her own behalf. And she had suggested—oh, it hardly bore thinking of—that he would marry some nit of a girl, and here he was expecting his possible wife-to-be at Nimmitibel on a visit!

She thought no more about what he had said regarding her coming to Nimmitibel to cook until past sundown. She was waiting in the car while the others said goodbye to various friends when he appeared and came to speak to her. She was so busy trying to think up some way of putting her apology into words that at first she didn't realize what he was saying.

"Well, Rennald Baxter—I've been talking to Meg and you're obviously out of a job at Silver Springs if cooking's your thing. So how about coming over to Nimmitibel to cook for me? I'm expecting a couple of houseguests and I don't imagine for a moment that they'll find my present kitchen arrangements anything like adequate.''

Rennie, slowly taking in what he had said, stared at him speechlessly. Those blue eyes were looking at her frankly, and there was a definite invitation in their depths, an invitation that she was certain had nothing at all to do with cooking. A couple of houseguests, he had put it. She thanked heaven that she just happened to know that one of those houseguests was the girl with whom he had fallen in love. He was, she decided, the same as any other man—and no doubt quite as devious as Pete and as ready to amuse himself with someone else on the side. As faithless as Jean-Yves, the other man in Rennie's life, who, though she had not known it until she had fallen well and truly in love with him, was going to marry another girl. "For family and financial reasons, you understand, *chérie*, I must go on with it. But it need not matter to us—we can still love. Clemence is a sophisticated girl. She will know when to turn the blind eye—''

And now here was this Outback man, obviously planning to work his undoubted charm on her to force her to withdraw her opinion of men in general and of him in particular, to eat her words, to fall under his spell. He would have a little affair with the cook oh, men were the same the world over, she thought angrily. But she was far from being an easy victim even to a man as formidable as himself, if he only knew it, and what was more, she was glad she had been rude to him and that there was not the least need anymore for her to apologize or to take back a single one of her remarks.

She told him briefly, coldly, definitely, "No, thank you, Mr. Deveraux. I'm not interested.''

He tilted an eyebrow. "Not interested? I thought you

wanted to see the Outback. You'll see a lot more of it at Nimmitibel than you will at Silver Springs."

"That may be so," she said dryly. "However, I have a job already—with your aunt. She pays me well, and I'm not silly enough to toss it in just to—" She stopped. Just to impress your girl friend and to amuse you, she might have said.

He looked at her consideringly. "Hmm. You have me there. I'll admit I wasn't offering you anything in the nature of a paying proposition. More a taste of Outback life. Could be you'd become addicted and change your mind about a lot of things, including me. You won't take it up?"

She shook her head and looked away from those blue, blue eyes that had suddenly narrowed, sharpened. "Definitely not."

"I'm disappointed. I guess talk is easier than action. You're a soft little English girl after all. It's too grim for you here. Too bad."

He turned away without even a goodbye. As far as he was concerned, her decision was final, and he didn't really care one way or the other. Rennie bit her lip and tried to analyze her own peculiarly mixed feelings. His taunt had annoyed her, and she hated to refuse a challenge. But exactly what sort of a challenge was it that he had tossed down? If she'd thought it was simply a case of whether or not the Outback was too tough for her, she would not have hesitated—she'd have taken him up at once. But there was this other thing. There was that invitation in his eyes. And she was not going to be made a fool of—to produce meals for another girl's enjoyment and to be offered some sort of intrigue on the side. She didn't want to play love games with anyone, be he boss or stockman. But was that what he had had in mind, or was she imagining it? He had, after all, suggested she might change her mind about him. . . .

Forget it, she told herself irritably. The others were coming back to the car. Tim looked very relaxed; he had his arm around Nancy's waist, and was obviously teasing her about her hat. Well, they at least were simple and uncomplicated.

For the next few days after that, the anticipated thrill of being in the Outback seemed to have gone sour on Rennie. It was as though she had been through some exhausting emotional experience at the picnic races, and it was an anticlimax the following day to steel herself to steer a diplomatic course between Meg Lang and Dr. Grace. She envied Nancy who was free to go out on the run with Tim each morning—and did so—while Rennie was left with the two older women and the giggling lubras in the big, half-empty homestead.

She seemed to listen interminably to Dr. Grace's comments on how the station was run, and on the stage of her digestion if she was compelled to eat many more dinners of steak and potatoes. Rennie would have liked to set to work in the kitchen and to immerse herself in practical activities, thereby dispelling all the vaguely troubling thoughts of Dev Deveraux and Nimmitibel cattle station from her mind. But Meg Lang didn't want her in her kitchen—and it was indubitably her kitchen, and had been so for many years. This was her home, even if to some degree she was working for Dr. Grace—and for Dev—and she had a right, Rennie was forced to acknowledge, to run it as she pleased.

It was a maddening position to be in, and Rennie couldn't understand why she didn't simply pack her bags and leave. Except that it was not as easy as that in the Outback.

Then one night she was actually allowed to get the

dinner all by herself as a special privilege, it seemed. Even the lubras who usually prepared the vegetables were banished from the kitchen and Rennie had it all to herself.

The meal turned out well, though it gave her little real satisfaction under the circumstances. Meg praised her and so, of course, did Dr. Grace—quite fulsomely. But Tim, while he said politely, "very nice," definitely did not approve. Cooking the dinner was his mother's responsibility, and Rennie knew that he disliked the idea of Dr. Grace getting her own way, throwing her weight around. He was no fool, and even if Dr. Grace had not told him as plainly as she had told Meg what her intentions were, he had obviously worked it out for himself.

He said that night, "If you've come out here to check me over, that's okay. But just let my mother get on with it, will you? This has been her home for a quarter of a century, even if her father didn't buy the property and build the homestead and stock the paddocks. She doesn't need anyone to teach her to cook, and we happen to like plain country food here. We don't hanker for fancy French dishes, even if you do, Dr. Warren."

Rennie heard this rather long speech as she came through to the veranda after going to her bedroom to freshen up her makeup—an excuse for a moment alone after the ordeal that dinner had become. They were having coffee out there, and Nancy had made it, offering to do so with a schoolgirlish ingenuity that Rennie suspected held a touch of diplomacy.

Hearing Tim's words, she flushed scarlet. If she had known her presence would prove such a bone of contention, then she would never have come to Silver Springs. But Dr. Grace had been so positive that they would all live on beef and damper without her that she had believed it.

She paused in the doorway for a moment to compose herself. "I'll leave tomorrow," she thought. "I'll manage it somehow."

Tim looked straight at her as she stepped into the light, and Nancy remarked lightly, "French cooking's out from now on, Rennie—except for Mother's vote. I'm glad I only made the coffee and that nobody started yelling for billy tea."

Tim gave a grunt and rose to stand against the veranda rail and look into the warm darkness of the night. Meg was plainly ill at ease. She doted on her son, but as well, she had a proper respect for Dr. Grace, ingrained no doubt from the days when her husband was a stockman on the property, and the strong-willed old man was boss.

Dr. Grace, however, was quite unperturbed. "It's absurd to have all this fuss simply because I've brought my cook along with me. It would do your mother no harm at all to have a rest from the cooking, Tim. I don't suppose she's had a holiday in years. I'm as well aware as anyone that father was a tyrant. . . . I'll have some more coffee, please, Nancy, and Rennald before you sit down you might see if I've left my cigarillos in the sitting room."

Rennie turned back. Right now she hated her position, her nonexistent job. Dr. Grace had no idea of tact her way was the right way, and that was all there was to it. Fleetingly, uselessly, she thought of Dev Deveraux's suggestion that she should come to Nimmitibel to cook, and she almost wished she had accepted it. Anything, it seemed just now, would be better than this.

She was hunting for the cigarillos when Nancy came through the sitting room with the coffee.

"I hope you're not upset, Rennie. Mother just likes to

have her own way. She's deliberately aggravating Tim she thinks it will make it easier to get rid of him.''

"Then I wish she wouldn't use me to attain her ends,'' said Rennie. "I'm beginning to wonder what I'm doing here—and to wish I hadn't come.''

"Well, now you're here you'll have to stay till Mother goes,'' said Nancy with callous cheerfulness. "If I were you, I'd forget about being conscientious and just have a good time. Why don't you come out on the ranch in the morning? Tim won't bite you he's quite fun really. Do you ride?''

"A little. But I don't think well enough for that—I'd be a drag.'' Rennie was pulled in two directions. She would have loved to do as Nancy suggested. But Dr. Grace was paying her and how did she get over that, seeing that she unfortunately had a conscience?

She found the cigarillos and followed Nancy on to the veranda, then restlessly went down the steps into the garden and began to walk slowly along the shadowy, scented path. The sky above was huge and dark and moon washed. Pink roses looked white, and red roses looked mysteriously blue. There were little rustlings and scurryings in the bushes, crickets chirped and an owl a long way off uttered an eerie cry—"Mopoke! Mopoke!'' Beyond the garden, the cattle country stretched endlessly, a strange flat plain that just now seemed to be a sea of billowing blue bush that moved and swelled almost imperceptibly under the light of the moon. Somewhere not far away there was the silver streak of water, the springs from which the station took its name, and where there was always fresh cool water.

The night was warm and soft and so untouched that Rennie stood perfectly still by the fence to let its spirit flood into her being. It would all work out—the thing was to relax, to accept, not to fight or get uptight or look for

trouble. Vaguely she was sorry for what she had said to
Dev Deveraux. And if she had said those same things to
Jake Ridley she would still have been sorry. Hitting out
might make you feel great at the time—and she was a girl
who had always hit out—but right now it seemed rather
petty.

As for her job, it had turned out to be not a job at all.
The simplest thing would be to ask Dr. Grace to release
her.

And yet she knew she did not want to go. She began to
think about Dev Deveraux again, and of the girl he had
invited to Nimmitibel. She knew that unless she cleared
out, she would see him again. Dr. Grace had said that
they would go to Nimmitibel for a short time at least,
and of course she would be taken along, too. She shivered
a little as the thought. She found she could call up his
image with a peculiar clarity—the blueness of his eyes,
his thick brown healthy-looking hair that waved slightly
as it fell over his square brow, the curl at the corners of
his mouth. Was he really living in the rough at Nimmitibel or was Dr. Grace exaggerating? And what was this
girl like, whom he had invited to his home? Would she
want to live there? Or would she join forces with Dr.
Grace and try to persuade Dev to move over to Silver
Springs?

And if he did move, what would become of the Langs?

She stirred and began to wander slowly back toward
the homestead. "Not my problem," she told herself
determinedly, annoyed that she had broken her tranquil
mood by thinking of Dev Deveraux and all that went
with him. And yet she knew that she could not bear the
thought of leaving the Outback till she had learned the
outcome of all these questions. True enough, she had
ceased to brood over her own dissatisfaction, but her
mind was by no means at rest. Instead, she felt nervous

and tense. All her senses seemed to be tuned up like the strings of a violin—the merest touch and she did not know what strange chord would send its vibrations into the air.

She returned to the homestead and found to her relief that there was now no one sitting on the veranda. Voices from the direction of the orange grove suggested that Nancy and Tim were there, and a couple of lights shining from doors farther along the veranda told her that both Dr. Grace and Meg Lang had gone to their bedrooms. A single soft light shone from the sitting room, and Rennie stood in the doorway and looked inside.

It was a lovely room with heavy dull-gold curtains and an almost new ivory-colored wallpaper that made an elegant background for the long sofa and several chairs covered in jade-green brocade. There were two beautiful carved and polish cedar tables and a writing table to match, and some small rugs of Indian design were scattered on the dark polished floor. It was a gracious room that had never been allowed to grow shabby or negelected, and Meg arranged fresh flowers there every day. Rennie imagined it must have been very much the same long ago when Grace Warren was still Grace Deveraux and had lived here with her father and her brother, Dev's father. Rennie could almost hear the laughter, the talk, the melody drifting from the piano by the far wall. . . .

Some faint movement drew her eyes from the piano to the mirror that hung on the wall to the left, and she was startled to see a tall slim girl standing there, hands raised to the straight shining blond hair that she was lifting from her neck. She wore a long apple-green gown, and Rennie caught the flash of light blue eyes that looked through the mirror with a bright intensity at—her? Or was it at someone behind her?

She glanced almost nervously over her shoulder. No one. Only the empty doorway.

And when she looked back the girl had gone. Soundlessly, as if she had never been there. Rennie blinked hard and felt a shiver pass through her. It was all her crazy imagination. She didn't believe in ghosts. But there was not a sound, and there was no one there. No one had ever been there. She bit her lip and turned away, walked quickly around the veranda to her bedroom. Once before she had thought she had seen a ghost—a girl in the sky on her last parachute jump. It was Pete Morgan's girl, whom she had met for the first time before the Cessna took off. "My fiancée, Susie Rainer," Pete had said, and Rennie had looked into the smiling brown eyes of the girl who stood on the airfield, and she had fainted—died—inwardly. "Wish you were coming up with us, Susie?" Pete had asked. And the girl had made a rueful face. "No more jumping for me—I promised daddy."

And later, when they were airborne—Rennie remembered it all painfully as she walked blindly into the dark warmth of her bedroom on an Outback cattle station in South Australia—later, Pete had said casually, almost playfully, "You'll have a new jump instructor next weekend, love. I'll be on my honeymoon." When she prepared to jump into the sky that afternoon she hadn't cared about anything—not anything at all. Her world had ended. Yet something within her, some proud spirit, had kept her from breaking down, from showing the hurt in her heart. "Make this the best jump you've ever done for me," Pete had said with his bright encouraging smile, and she knew he was watching her to see that she was in the right frame of mind for a jump. He was always scrupulously careful that way, and she wondered whether he had any idea that meeting Susie Rainer might have been in the nature of a traumatic experience.

Later, because Pete pretty well took it for granted that she had jumped with the intention of destroying herself, she believed he had known. And certainly when she jumped she had been in despair. She had thought of Jean-Yves and she had tensed at the thought of going through all that anguish again. And then miraculously, wonderfully she discovered that she had flung out her arms and legs and arched her back. She was in the stable position and counting the seconds as Pete had taught her to do. She had pulled the ripcord, felt the jerk as the canopy began to flower over her head. Her legs had swung down and she had known once more the indescribable exhilaration and awe the sense of absolute freedom of being upheld by the invisible arms of the air as she looked down on the beautiful, beautiful green world spread out beneath her.

She heard a church bell chime. The sound floated past her and then was gone, and there was only silence as she swung high in space away from everyone and everything. Except that up in the Cessna Pete was watching her, assessing her performance. *My last jump for Pete,* she thought with an almost dispassionate bitterness. On her own in the sky, the bitterness was like the bite of a single stinging drop of acid, a shining poisoned jeweled asp to be contemplated aloofly as though it concerned someone who belonged on the solid, workaday world. Not Rennie, as she swung untouchable between heaven and earth.

Somewhere in the next few seconds an eerie and incredible thing had happened—the thing she had never been able to confess to anyone, not even to Pete to absolve him from the feeling of guilt that she had lost her head because of him. For an infinitesimal fraction of time, another girl swung beside her—a girl in parachuting gear, in boots and helmet, but without goggles so that Rennie saw clearly her shining brown eyes and the smile on her lips. She was floating down as Rennie was, and then, quite simply, she was gone.

How long had it taken? No time at all. Yet Rennie's equilibrium was completely upset in that unnerving inexplicable instant. She lost every scrap of her ordinarily automatic concentration. For some mad reason she had pulled—hard—on her left toggle, swung around, looked down and discovered she was running with the wind and way off course, with the ground coming closer and closer. She didn't panic, but her mind was muddled. She couldn't think quickly and by the time she realized what she should have done it was too late. She was coming down in a clump of trees. She shielded her face as she had been taught to do, but it was not good enough. She was lucky not to have damaged her eyes. She could feel the blood running down her cheek as she hung in the tree waiting for someone to come and get her down, and she felt cold and shaken.

Remembering it all now had sent her hands to her face. She could feel her scar burning, and she could hear a drawling voice asking her, "How did *that* happen?"

"Stop it!" Had she said it aloud? And why was she standing here in the dark?

She moved stiffly and switched on the light. If there was a ghost at Silver Springs cattle station, it was nothing to do with Rennald Baxter. Thank goodness for that.

She asked Meg about it the next day, but casually, noncommittally, not giving herself away.

"Do you have a ghost here, Mrs. Lang?"

"A ghost? Dear me, no—nothing as romantic as that, dear. I'm afraid I don't believe in ghosts in any case. Do you?"

She looked and sounded amused, and Rennie said sturdily, "No, of course I don't," and then Dr. Grace had come in. Rennie forgot all about ghosts and tried to hand in her resignation.

"Dr. Grace, I would like to go back to Adelaide. There's no job for me here and you can't pay me for doing nothing."

Dr. Grace looked at her frowningly. "Oh, don't talk such nonsense, Rennald. You can't go back to Adelaide, that should be obvious to you. And having brought you all this way, I don't intend to lose you. Just dig your toes in and Meg will let you help her in the kitchen. But don't make a fuss, for goodness' sake, I've other things to think of besides your complaints."

Rennie grimaced inwardly and stalked off rebelliously. She wondered with a little feeling of depression just how long she would be able to put up with this inactivity.

That night after dinner her spirits were raised. Tim, who had been in the office ringing through to Nimmitibel, came back to the veranda with the news that Dev's visitors had arrived the previous evening. And having tossed down this conversational bait, he gathered up Nancy and they departed for a turn around the garden, leaving Meg, Dr. Grace and Rennie to indulge in whatever feminine speculation they liked.

"I'm so glad for Dev," said Meg animatedly. "I remember saying when Isobel was here and she and Dev had met for the first time, 'I sense a love match there.' They were very much taken up with each other from the word go. She and Lynette work on the same paper in Adelaide, and she's a very pretty girl, but clever and worldly, too. So exactly right for someone as strongly masculine and demanding as Dev."

Dr. Grace lit a cigarillo and leaned back in her chair.

"Tim will have to start looking for another management."

The other woman smiled comfortably. "I don't think so. I don't think we'll be uprooting ourselves from here. Dev has complete faith in Tim."

"That," said Dr. Grace, amused, "is scarely the point."

Rennie quietly collected the coffee cups and took them out to the kitchen. As she washed them, she wondered what difference she expected Tim's news to make in her life, for she was filled with a vague sense of excitement. She certainly felt very curious about this girl of Dev Deveraux's and longed to meet her. She was glad now that Dr. Grace had paid so little attention to her when she had said she wanted to leave. Imagine being back in Adelaide now, looking for another job and not having the least idea what was happening out here in this part of the cattle country! How deadly dull!

When she went back inside, everyone was gathered in the sitting room, and Rennie was just in time to hear Dr. Grace remarking, "Tomorrow morning I'll drive over to Nimmitibel and stay for a few days."

Rennie's heart gave a leap, and Nancy, who was sorting over a pile of stereo records with Tim at the far end of the room, for they had decided to dance on the veranda, looked up to say, "Well, I'm not coming, mother. You can have it all on your own. I'm staying here in comfort."

"Please yourself," said her mother indifferently. She looked at Rennie, who discovered she was standing with tightly clenched fists, her heart beating hard. Without a doubt, she would be going to Nimmitibel, too. Dr. Grace wouldn't want to rough it more than need be, and Dev himself had admitted that his kitchen arrangements left a lot to be desired. She thought, "At all events, I'll make it clear from the start that he can't play games with me. I'll show him I meant every word I said. I'm not even vaguely interested in Outback men—Dev Deveraux in particular. . . ."

She was positively stunned when Dr. Grace said, "You might as well stay here too, Rennald. Nimmitibel is primitive. I won't subject you to it."

Rennie's mouth fell open and she knew an unbelievable feeling of disppointment and letdown. "But," she stammered, "you'll need me there to do the cooking—"

"I'll put up with the existing conditions," said Dr. Grace placidly. "Dev might be insulted if I brought my own cook along—he's so damned proud and pigheaded he considers his household arrangements are all anyone could wish."

"But he doesn't—he asked me to come himself," Rennie wanted to say. But of course she didn't. It struck her suddenly that Dr. Grace had a good reason for deciding to dispense with her services. It wouldn't help the doctor's cause to have life at Nimmitibel made more comfortable for Isobel. She, Rennie, was positively the last person to be considered in this setup. It didn't matter in the least to anyone that she had come out here to do a job and that she was not being allowed to do it. She flashed out, "I'm beginning to wonder why you ever brought me along with you."

"Oh, count your blessings, Rennald. You're getting your money and you're having a holiday. Make the most of your good luck."

How? thought Rennie furiously. Tim had put a pop record on the player and he and Nancy were dancing on the veranda and laughing together, enjoying themselves. Rennie felt utterly frustrated. She didn't know how she was expected to amuse herself all on her own. She suddenly reflected that she hadn't even met the handsome Jake Ridley yet and dealt him the treatment he deserved. And now it didn't look as though she ever would. And she was right in the mood to tell some man exactly what she thought of the male sex. . . .

Dr. Grace left the following morning, driving too fast and followed by a cloud of dust. Rennie watched until her car had disappeared around the long hill beyond the homestead. What now? Nancy as usual was out with Tim, so she went down to the saddling yards and asked the lanky shy stockman there to saddle up a nice safe horse for her, and she went out for a ride.

It was very hot and the air felt dry as dust and she hadn't any idea where to go. She followed a track there were several of them radiating out from the homestead. The track she picked led past the horse paddock toward a fence with a gate that had to be opened. Ahead, it went straight across a singularly flat section of the property, and a couple of miles off though it was hard to judge distances in the shimmering vibrating air where water mirages danced everywhere on the horizon there was a silvery shed that looked to Rennie very much like a hangar. It probably was. She knew that men on the Outback station sometimes used planes for checking bores and water holes and even for mustering stock. She rode on with a feeling of eagerness, curious to see whether or not there was a plane out there.

There was. And it was a Cessna 172.

Rennie left her horse in the shade of a small group of trees close to the hangar and went in to look at the Cessna. It gave her a very curious feeling to be looking at a plane this close once more—a plane this size. It was nothing like the enormous jet she had flown out from England in. This was the type of plane they had used at the parachuting club. A feeling of nostagia and excitement rose in her and her legs shook a little as she walked around the plane. There was complete silence in the shed and all around except for the ticking of the iron roof in the heat. She felt she was in some kind of dream, and she walked uncertainly, cautiously, almost as if she expected to see another ghost—perhaps Pete's—here in the hangar.

She didn't see a ghost. But she became aware of something that was in a way quite as startling as a ghost would have been: this plane had had its starboard door and its wheel spats removed. The seat next to the pilot's had been taken out.

Rennie felt a kind of faintness overtake her. She must be dreaming—or else she was seeing things. Why on earth would a plane so obviously prepared for parachute jumping be here in a hangar in the Outback? But it was here all right. She touched it—she climbed inside. And she was aware of a feeling that was a combination of nausea and an almost intolerable excitement. To jump again—to be free in the air—

She had believed that day she said goodbye to parachute jumping—could it possibly be just under three months ago—that she would never ever want to jump again. But it was a bug, an addiction, that was tenacious. Perhaps partly because just now her life was so curiously a vacuum, so completely without adventure, without challenge, without love—she wanted more than anything to get into her parachuting gear, to launch herself into space, to be back in the familar element, maneuvering her descent skillfully, watching the target coming closer.

She blinked hard and found she was actually blinking away tears. Then she walked out again into the blinding, dazzling sunlight. Quite probably this plane had been bought secondhand from a parachuting club. She didn't imagine that the old man had been a skydiver. Or Tim. No, for some reason she was certain that skydiving was not in Tim Lang's line at all. He was steady, and dependable.

She caught her horse got into the saddle, and rode back to the homestead.

That afternoon some people from Utmaowie station called at Silver Springs—Mrs. Simpson, who was seventy or so, and her daughter-in-law Olive, both of whom Rennie had met briefly at the picnic races. They were full of gossip about Dev Deveraux's visitors and the possibility of a wedding in the district in the near future. Rennie, feeling it did not concern her, excused herself, saying she had letters to write. But she heard as she made her departure, "It will take a clever girl to rope Dev in. He's always been wild, untamable."

Meg Lang said placidly, "Isobel Sandison is a clever girl—"

Rennie grimaced. Isobel Sandison was welcome to her wild untamable man! As for herself—she'd rather take up mountain climbing or deep-sea diving or something. Only next time she would keep her heart out of it.

The telephone rang that night as she was passing the office door and she answered it without thinking.

"Who's that?" a male voice rapped out sharply. She recognized it instantly as Dev Deveraux's voice, and though she tensed, her heart gave an unsteady jog.

"Rennald Baxter. Who is that?"

He didn't bother to answer. He said, "So, you're still there. I thought you'd have run away—chickened out. Get Tim for me, will you?"

"Certainly," said Rennie, chilled by the coolness, the complete indifference of his voice. She suddenly doubted herself—wondered if she had dreamed up all those ulterior motives she had suspected when he had invited her to Nimmitibel. Certainly right now he didn't sound as if he had the least possible personal interest in her. And that phrase chickened out was one that she did not like.

Instead of going to fetch Tim, she heard herself ask him with a sort of frigid politeness, "How are your guests making out?"

"They're having a hell of a time. And that includes Grace. They find the food unspeakable. It's a great pity you proved to be such a little hothouse plant you couldn't come over. You can't expect to see much of the Outback if you stay under glass. Despite your showy words of the other day, I can see you're scared to death of my country."

"Can you?" she said coldly, though her heart was hammering. "Well, I can't help what you believe of me, Mr. Deveraux, and I really don't care very much. I'm here on a job and I do as I'm told."

"It's easy money, isn't it?" He paused and she said nothing. She simply felt furiously angry. "Now go and fetch Tim, will you?"

She didn't answer. She went and fetched Tim and then she stood alone on the veranda, her back to the house, fuming.

Oh, but it went against the grain to have her valor, her nerve, her backbone discounted. To be passed off as some weakling who couldn't take the Outback. Scared of his country! She was not one bit intimidated by the Outback or by anything in it. In fact, she very much wanted to see Nimmitibel. The only fly in the ointment was that Nimmitibel meant Dev Deveraux. And if she hadn't learned from experience to distrust the human male, she would have taken up his challenge like a shot and gone to cook for him, his girl friend, his stockmen and anyone else who might come over the horizon. But now she seriously began to doubt her interpretation of the challenge he had tossed her that day at the picnic races. He was not interested in playing games with her. That was only what her own suspicious mind had suggested to her. He had simply been challenging her professed interest in the Outback. And now he thought she was fainthearted, a namby-pamby.

She heard Tim come back into the sitting room and tell his mother and Nancy, "Dev wants me to fly the Cessna up tomorrow—take a look over the far northeastern paddock at Nimmity and put the plane down on his strip. Like to come along, Nancy?"

"It would be super," Nancy agreed with enthusiasm.

Tim came to the door. "You there, Rennie? Dr. Grace is staying on a while, and it seems she wants her personal cook at Nimmitibel after all—unless you've made up your mind to leave us altogether?"

Rennie was suddenly alert. "Of course I haven't." Dev, she supposed, had put that idea into his mind.

"Great. How about coming in the Cessna, then? Or are you scared of small planes?"

Rennie smiled wryly. "Why would I be?"

"Dev thinks you might be. And let's face it, you're—well, not one of us." He looked suddenly embarrassed.

"A hothouse flower," said Rennie brightly, and he looked more embarrassed than ever.

"You're a domesticated sort of girl," he said lamely. "That's what I meant. Not an outdoor type. Dev says if you don't want to do the trip in the Cessna, don't think you have to."

Dev says! Rennie's sea-blue eyes sparked. "If Dr. Grace wants me, I certainly have to," she snapped. She felt infuriated. To be belittled like that—by Dev, of course, it was all Dev. She would dearly love to show him just how mistaken he was about this little domesticated English girl, this hothouse plant. Scared of "his" country, scared of the Cessna! She said with sudden briskness,

"I took a look at the Cessna this morning, as a matter of fact. It's been used for parachute jumping at some time or another, hasn't it?"

Tim's look of astonishment almost made her laugh. His gray eyes had opened wide, and Nancy, who had come to lounge beside him in the doorway, leaning comfortably against his shoulder, said, "How on earth would you know that, Rennie?"

"It's obvious to anyone who's been involved in the sport," said Rennie matter-of-factly. "Who does the parachuting around here?"

She more or less expected to be told, no one. Instead, Tim said, "Dev, of course," and she didn't know why, but she felt prickles run up and down her spine and she wanted to laugh. Dev again! "He belongs to a parachuting club," Tim said. "At least he used to till lately. His equipment's still here in the hangar, as a matter of fact. But I don't expect he wants it taken to Nimmitibel. He's given it up."

"Jumping?"

"Yes."

"Since when? And why?"

"Since roughly a month ago," said Tim, obviously surprised at her questions. "As for why too long between jumps, too far to the club." He shrugged. "I don't know. Too much to keep him busy at Nimmitibel."

"Besides which," came Meg's voice from inside, "it's a dangerous sport and it wouldn't be fair to Isobel. I've been trying to get him to promise to give it up for a long time."

Nancy was still staring at Rennie. "Don't tell me you parachuted, Rennie! I'd never have the nerve. I'd be scared stiff."

"So is everyone," said Rennie with a casual smile. She was thinking of that equipment out at the hanger recently used, surely serviceable. . . . She said, not wanting to talk about herself or her past, "Well—I'll go tomorrow. I'm a cook, and if Dr. Grace wants me, I'm ready and willing to work."

That was the end of the matter. But when she went to bed that night, she lay awake a long time thinking of that parachuting gear lying out at the hanger not much more than two miles away.

CHAPTER THREE

SOMETIME DURING THE NIGHT and not altogether consciously, Rennie decided what she was going to do. She was going to persuade Tim to let her jump over Nimmitibel—so long as there was a suitable dropping zone and the wind was not blowing a gale.

She was up early in the morning, she got herself some breakfast and she rode out to the hangar to take a look at Dev's equipment. The chute was neatly packed and it looked ready for jumping, but Rennie had been scrupulously taught to take no chances. If Dev didn't intend to jump again—for whatever reason, consideration for Isobel or anything else—it could be that his gear was unserviceable—a tear here, a strap missing, you never knew. She unpacked it and examined it thoroughly, checking for faults. Everything was in order, and she set about the task of repacking, taking her time and making a thorough job of it. Packing was important. She had pushed the last pin home and was tucking in the loose flap ends when Tim came into the hangar.

"What are you doing with that gear?" he asked sharply.

She answered calmly, "I've been checking it over. It's in perfect order. I thought it would be fun if you'd drop me down over Nimmitibel today."

His mouth opened soundlessly and she smiled at him beguilingly. "Please, Tim. I'm not asking you to do anything risky. I've done a lot of jumping. As a matter of fact, I can show you my log book. It's a beautifully calm day and it shouldn't be all that hard out here to find a nice open space free of telegraph wires and skyscrapers and deep water. There's an airstrip at Nimmitibel, isn't there? That should be ideal.''

He shook his head stubbornly. "I'm not going to drop you down on it. You can come down in the plane with me and Nancy. What's the big idea, asking me to do a thing like that?''

She made a little rueful face. "The idea is—I love jumping, that's all. I'm just itching to jump. And it will be perfectly safe honestly. I can tell you exactly what I want you to do once I've seen the landing strip. I'll tell you when to cut out the engine—everything. And I promise you faithfully I'll take no chances. I value my life too much to do that.''

"No,'' said Tim.

"Why not? Because you're afraid of Dev?'' she reasoned. "Is he a sort of mastermind in your life? Can't you make any decisions of your own?'' She looked at him hard with just a tinge of mockery in her eyes. "Are you afraid he'll use it as an excuse to throw you out of Silver Springs and move in himself? Dr. Grace says that's what he intends to do anyhow—''

"My *foot*,'' said Tim. "I'm here because I know how to run the place, and Dev stays on Nimmitibel because it's his kind of country. . . . In any case, he just doesn't come into this.''

"Great,'' said Rennie. She picked up her log book— she had brought it with her—and handed it to him. She was quite sure that if he looked through it carefully and read her instructor's comments he would have complete faith in her. She was silent for five minutes while he examined the log book, and then he looked up straight at her.

"You're a surprising girl," was all he said. But she knew she had won her point. And when he remarked casually as they went back to the homestead together, "I don't think we'll mention this to my mother, if you don't mind," she agreed equally casually.

Looking down from a plane on the Outback country, she discovered some two hours later, was very different from looking down on the green fields of England. The air was hot and still, and she looked forward to a long slow ride down through the sky, particularly since she didn't have her heavy boots on and had chosen instead the most sensible and sturdy shoes she had brought with her. She was filled with a heady sense of excitement and beneath it all she was disturbingly aware that she badly wanted to show Mr. Deveraux that she was far from being the timid, sheltered, unadventurous girl he chose to believe.

She had taken up her position on the floor near the pilot's seat, and she quietly briefed Tim on what would be expected of him and why. Nancy, in the passenger seat behind, was singularly quiet. She was a little apprehensive about Rennie's jumping.

"I wish you wouldn't," she had said weakly as she had watched Rennie getting into the unwieldy-looking gear back in the hangar, but after that, she had held her tongue.

Now Rennie watched from the empty doorway as the world slid away far below. They flew over mile after mile of straw-colored carpet patterned in gray green and gray blue, channeled here and there by riverbeds where the occasional gleam of water reflecting the blue of the skies flashed brightly. She saw a huge mob of cattle by some tiny yards, and among the trees moving dots that must be cattle, too. And then, after a while, the face of the land changed, and down below there was bare earth of a singing red color, billowing in long low waves and scattered with long drifts and small round clusters of gray green trees—the mulga.

Soon there was the unexpected sight of a thick belt of trees fringing a long broken erratic strip of water. On one side of the water was a cluster of buildings with a line drawn around it that must be a fence. Nancy said, "That's Nimmitibel—your destination. Lucky you—I don't think!"

Rennie stared down, searching for tiny figures but seeing none. She caught herself thinking, It will be a bit of an anticlimax if he doesn't even see me coming down! Quickly, she pushed that thought aside. She could see the airstrip now, hard, sunbaked red earth—no soft green grassy dropping zone here. There was a tiny hangar at one end and quite plainly to be seen, wheel tracks scarring out from the home paddock. No hazards, she assessed, and the wind just didn't seem to exist. She let Tim take the plane over the airstrip and then directed him to turn and fly back again. Carefully, she eased herself into position by the door.

"I'll tell you exactly when to cut the engine," she told Tim, "and then I'll be on my way. And please," she added quickly, aware that at this last minute he was having doubts, "don't tell me you won't play. I'm all dressed up and ready and I'll be perfectly safe."

Less than a minute later she was shouting, as she had so often heard Pete shouting, "Cut!" and then she felt the whip of the slipstream as she dropped away, arms and legs flung out, head up, silently counting out the seconds before she pulled the ripcord.

Then there was the familiar jerk on her shoulders, her legs swung down, she grasped the risers and looked up to

see the canopy above her, unfolding, blossoming, filling
with air. She pulled gently on one toggle so that she
swung around, looked down and saw the red of the
airstrip stretching out below. She was moving slowly,
smoothly, and it was heavenly indescribably heavenly.
And easy! Oh, she had never had it so easy! There was
simply nothing to jumping when the air was still like this
and there was all that space below to land on, and the
heat rising from the sunbaked land slowed down her rate
of descent to an absolute minimum. She felt herself so
gently uplifted, upheld by the wings of the air wafted,
whispered to oh, in the heavenly sky! She felt like
writing poetry—

A bird drifted past like a bright leaf red and yellow
and green. She had never met such a bird in the sky
before! She swung herself around a little so that she
could see the Nimmitibel homestead, and now there was
a small group of people outside the garden looking up at
her, and except for the fact that she was holding the
steering toggles, she would have liked to give them a
cheery wave. She felt very free and unencumbered without goggles, despite the helmet – which was a must when
you were coming down on hard earth as she was going to
do. The one thing that irked her a little was that it was all
so easy there was just no chance at all to exercise any
skill.

Here, she discerned just two seconds later, she was
quite wrong. For suddenly something was rushing up to
meet her from the earth below. A red shadow raced
madly across the red sand, a red giant flung itself shaking
and quaking into the sunny silence of the air, and Rennie
felt her canopy rock.

A whirlwind!

As if by some fiendish conjuring trick, the monster
extended itself to an enormous height and started reeling

toward her through the sky, throwing handfuls of leaves and dust and debris about itself with a gruesome prodigality.

Rennie made a mighty effort to collect her scattered senses. She pulled on one toggle to change course and the monster changed course too. Now she tacked to the right, and again the whirlwind followed. She felt a panicky certainty that it was out to get her, and she hadn't the faintest notion what to do. All too vividly she could picture herself caught up—dizzied—her canopy ripped to shreds, her body dropping like a stone. She looked down at the red earth below, and the next second she was whipped up by a wind that had come from nowhere. Before her eyes the whirlwind sank whimpering to nothingness on the ground, while she skimmed speedily on, over the airstrip, over the trees beyond—

She was coming down fast into a patch of mulga—no, she was going to miss it—there was an open stretch of ground beyond. She skimmed the trees, she tucked in her elbows, put her head well down on her chest, brought her feet and knees together and forced herself somehow to relax. And then she had landed, managing a side roll marred only by the fact that as her left shoulder hit the ground something sharp ripped the sleeve of her cotton shirt and stung into her flesh. Then she had completed her roll, jumped to her feet and automatically run around the canopy to collapse it.

She felt slightly dazed, but stimulated, too—exhilarated now that it was all over and she was safe. She felt grateful that she hadn't ripped the canopy. There was quite a large clear space around her, and by some miracle she had come to no harm at all, except that a sharp stick had savaged her upper arm. One part of her wanted to be back in the sky again so that she could deal with that whirlwind in some other way. It was always like that after you came down you wanted to go back. But now she pulled off her helmet and began to get out of her equipment. She had a long walk ahead of her unless someone drove out from the homestead to pick her up— and she was not taking that for granted. The easiest way to carry the 'chute was to field pack it, and this she proceeded to do, beginning by laying the canopy out in a good straight line. She certainly didn't want to cause trouble for herself with Dev Deveraux by messing up the gear that she had borrowed without his permission, and later on she would check over it very thoroughly.

She was busy chaining the rigging lines when something made her look up.

A man stood watching her from halfway across the clearing. A stockman, obviously, broad-brimmed hat tilted forward over his suntanned face. He wore a checked shirt and dusty, narrow-legged trousers, and his feet were clad in dusty stockmen's boots. He tossed down the cigarette he had been smoking, ground it out with one of those boots and came toward her.

Rennie stared. He was crazily, incredibly handsome, like someone out of a movie. In full color. His eyes were a startling yellow green. She had never seen such eyes before—long and clear and black lashed to match his hair. And as hard as stones. She thought instantly, "He's not quite human."

Then she drew a deep breath. It was Jake Ridley, of course!

"So it's a female," he drawled. "When I saw you skimming over the trees there, I thought you were a boy. . . . What the hell are you up to?"

"I'm packing this chute," said Rennie, and proceeded to get on with it.

"And after that?" he insisted.

She looked up at him, coolly quizzical, she asked

"Does it matter all that much? What's worrying you, anyhow? Are you afraid I might ask you to take me to your bungalow so I can get out of this messy gear and look cute in a pair of your pajamas? Or your bathrobe?"

A glimmer of surprise lit his stone cold eyes. He said evenly, "I don't own a pair of pajamas. Or a bathrobe. Or, come to that, a bungalow either."

"Well then, that lets us both out," said Rennie, getting on with her packing. It should get home to him pretty quickly that *this* female wasn't interested in him.

He said nothing more. He watched her in silence until she had completed her pack, slung it over her shoulders and fastened the chest strap. Then he remarked neutrally, "You should get that cut on your arm fixed up. It could turn septic."

She shrugged. "I'll do that when I get back to civilization."

"Civilization? Adelaide?"

"Nimmitibel homestead."

"Is that where you're heading?"

"What do you think? I didn't decide to drop out of the sky on this particular spot by chance."

"No? I rather thought that whirlwind chased you here."

She smiled fractionally. "All right. I am a little off course," she agreed.

"Just as well you didn't come down in the middle of the muster. I'd have had a stampede on my hands. . . . Who are you by the way?"

"No one you've ever heard of. The new cook for Nimmitibel," she said rashly. She had introduced herself as the cook once before to someone whom she had thought to be Jake Ridley, now she was trying it again. But she didn't have the same impassioned feeling about him any longer, somehow. She couldn't be bothered trying to avenge Nancy. It was enough to be cool, offhand. And it was the way she liked to be. He could take it or leave it. And then she wondered if she could have made another mistake. She asked hesitatingly, "You're Jake Ridley, aren't you?"

"Who told you?"

She shrugged. "I just guessed the head stockman, you know. I'm Rennald Baxter." She put out her hand and he took it, and that was the moment when a jeep came into the clearing, screeched to a stop and disgorged the boss of Nimmitibel cattle ranch.

In two seconds he was glowering down at Rennie who had managed to disengage her hand from Jake Ridley's. Looking at him, she felt her face grow white. He looked angry enough to kill her.

"So it's you, Rennald Baxter," he said between his teeth. Rennie had read of men saying things between their teeth and now she was experiencing it. It was as though he could hardly get the words out for his rage. His blue eyes traveled over her while Jake Ridley stepped a little to one side and proceeded to light another cigarette. Rennie gave him a quick glance and saw the hard green of his eyes like a cold fire above the match flame. Then Dev had taken her by the arm and with fingers that were the opposite of gentle had pushed back her sleeve and revealed the gash that something sharp had made when she rolled over on the ground.

"Is this all the damage you've done?"

She nodded, and heard herself quavering, "The chute's fine. I'll check it over properly when I—"

"You'll do nothing until you've explained yourself to me," he interrupted. He gestured with his head at Jake and said grimly, "Get back to the muster, Jake. I'll take this girl back to the homestead and she can give me a full account of herself."

"Don't be too hard on her," said Jake laconically. "She's all right."

Rennie gave him an astonished look and so, she was aware, did Dev. But he turned his back and strode off into the mulga.

"Into the jeep," said Dev, still tight-lipped. His fingers were hurting her arm, and suddenly she felt just the slightest bit nauseated. She stood dead still.

"Please let go of my arm. What am I? A criminal?" He dropped his hand at once and she rubbed her upper arm where his fingers had left a red mark. The blood on her gash had dried, but it felt painful. She said almost querulously, "And stop talking about me giving an account of myself. I've come to cook for Dr. Grace."

Four seconds passed. Rennie knew four seconds by heart. It was the time you let go by before you opened your chute. Then he said, "Risking your neck so that my aunt can relish her food—what's the matter with you? Do you think I'm going to swallow such nonsense as that? You could have come down with Tim. That's what I—" He stopped speaking abruptly and began to move toward the jeep again, gesturing to her to go ahead of him. She went. She badly needed to sit down. She almost needed to cry—to shed just a few tears anyhow. She was after all—as Jake had said—a female. And she was reacting after some pretty high tension.

She climbed into the jeep and he slammed the door, walked around and got in beside her. Then he started up the motor, swung the vehicle furiously around, and followed by a cloud of red dust, they shot off along a non-existent track that was far bumpier than any she had traveled with Dr. Grace.

"Didn't it occur to you that you might just possibly kill yourself—or worse, cripple yourself?" he said presently. "On my property, and while making unsolicited use of my valuable equipment? Which might, for all you knew, have been completely unserviceable.''

''It wasn't. I checked,'' said Rennie defensively. ''And I haven't damaged it—''

He ignored her and continued to drive like a man possessed, so that she had to grip the edge of the seat to prevent herself from being thrown violently against him. It was hard enough at any rate to keep her balance in the clumsy equipment. Talk about taking risks! Was he trying to kill both of them?

''I've a good mind,'' he fumed on, ''to throw young Tim Lang out for such irresponsible behavior!''

''He wasn't to blame at all,'' said Rennie. Her cheeks were still white and she was trembling a little. Such a gigantic fuss about nothing at all! He was spoiling all the pleasure of her jump—a jump she would have liked to recollect in detail and in tranquillity, so that she could savor the good moments and analyze the bad ones. ''I told you I checked your equipment before I used it—I'm not a fool. And I produced my log book for Tim so that he could see I was well qualified to jump. He did nothing wrong at all. There were no hazards—'' Her voice trailed off. No hazards, only a giant whirlwind that had been bent on killing her—

She saw the corner of his mouth lift in a grim and unexpected smile, and she admitted, ''Well . . . that whirlwind. But that would never happen again. And if it did, I'd do better next time, I'd—''

''There damn well won't be a next time,'' he said with a shocking savagery. ''You will never—you hear me, *never*—lay hands on my equipment again. No matter what the circumstances. Nor will you use my aircraft as a possible jumping-off place for killing yourself. You've let me know already that you have some sort of kink when it comes to the male sex. Well, that's your business, but if it's bad enough to make you want to say goodbye to the world, you can do it somewhere else.''

"I'll try to remember,'' said Rennie coldly. It seemed the best she could manage.

When they pulled up outside the eight-foot-high wind-break of old man saltbush that surrounded the home-stead garden, she expected to be told she could go straight back to Silver Springs. And as she stepped out of the dusty jeep, feeling ludicrously clumsy with the para-chute pack still strapped to her body, and the helmet in one hand, he said, his nostrils white, "The wisest thing I could do right now would be to pack you off to Adelaide. We just don't have room for bloody-minded wildcat girls of your sort in this country.''

That was going too far, and Rennie put her chin up. "What *do* you want, then? Hothouse flowers are out— nothing pleases you.'' He didn't answer and she didn't blame him. It was a stupid thing to have said.

"But as you're here,'' he said, "you can damn well stay and earn your keep. We need a cook.''

He strode off and stood holding the gate open for her, and after a second's indecision she followed him. A cook. Why did she hate him for saying that? Hadn't she been going around telling everyone that she was the cook? And wasn't that why Dr. Grace had sent for her? Sea-blue eyes bright, she told him, "I'll pay for my keep if you like, Mr. Deveraux—out of my wages.'' And that, she was pleased to observe, made him look intensely annoyed.

He took her into the homestead through the kitchen. Not, she was fair enough to realize, because that was where she would be working, but because he didn't want anyone else around. It was almost lunchtime and a large cheerful-looking aboriginal woman in a blue cotton dress was busy at the stove. It was a black fuel stove, and the kitchen was enormous and devastatingly hot and separated from the main part of the house by a covered passageway. Rennie followed Dev through that and at any minute she expected to find herself in the office on the mat, as it were, and being asked to explain herself.

Instead, she was taken into a bathroom large, cool, with black and white tiles on the floor and walls and an enormous shower cubicle. True, it could all do with a good cleaning, but it was far from uncivilized. Dev opened a drawer in the small enameled chest that stood under a smeared-looking glass, took out cotton wool, gauze, a bandage and small bottle of antiseptic.

He helped her unfasten the parachute pack, then while she sat down on a stool, he dealt quickly and efficiently with her arm. Rennie sat passive and exhausted. His fingers were gentle, and she was thankful that he asked no questions and didn't make conversation, and she found herself staring at the face that was so close to hers but so completely unaware of her. It was strange that skin and hair could be so nearly the same color—and that a man's eyelashes could be so thick and tip-tilted and his eyes

Those eyes suddenly glanced at her as he asked clinically, kindly almost, "Stinging?"

She shook her head and finished her thought. His eyes so blue.

She rose as soon as he had fastened the bandage around her arm. "Thank you very much. It feels really comfortable. I'm sorry to have put you to so much trouble."

"Think nothing of it." His look was sardonic. "We can't have your wound turning septic."

Rennie prepared to move off. "I'll go and check your chute and repack it properly."

"You can do that later, out at the hangar where there's

room,'' he said. "Now I'm going to get you a brandy and you can see if you feel like joining the company.''

The company. His houseguests and Dr. Grace. Quite suddenly Rennie was conscious that she had behaved badly. She *had* implicated Tim; she had, to some extent, shown off—and that was very bad taste. You didn't jump to show off, it was the worst possible approach to the sport. But she had wanted to show off—for a while, at any rate. Until she had been in the air and the poetry of it all had caught her up. But this time she did owe him an apology.

She offered it in the dining room a rather bare long dining room, with dusty corners and absolutely none of the elegance of Silver Springs. She gulped down the brandy he had poured, and he watched her.

"That will put the stuffing back into you."

"Yes." She added with an effort, "I'm sorry I behaved as I did on your property. But please don't take it out on Tim."

His eyes were guarded. "How did you persuade him to act so irresponsibly, for God's sake? With your feminine charms, I presume—which you seemed to be exercising also on my head stockman. But him I would advise you to forget about. Remember that, will you?" He paused, waited, then rapped out, "Well—will you?" She nodded, and knew that the stuffing had not yet been put back into her. "Right. And now you'd better come inside or Grace will think you've been killed."

Rennie looked down at her dusty clothes with distaste.

"You'll have to wait till Tim brings your clothes before you can change," he said unsympathetically, following her glance. "That's part of the punishment for an unorthodox arrival. . . . He should have been here by now—he must be giving my young cousin quite a joyride, having disposed of you so neatly."

There were three people in the shabby sitting room when they went in. Dr. Grace and a small round-faced woman reclined in armchairs, while a tall slim girl, her back to the room, stood in the doorway that opened on to the veranda. Rennie was uncomfortably aware that the two older women were staring at her and that Dr. Grace looked far from delighted to see her. In fact, she asked in a tone of obvious displeasure, "What on earth are you doing here, Rennald? Don't tell me it was you we saw jump out of the Cessna."

"I assure you it was," said Dev dryly. Then, "Miss Sandison, Isobel this is Rennald Baxter who's come to cook for us. Rennald Miss Nina Sandison, Isobel Sandison."

The girl in the doorway, who had turned slightly, now faced into the room, and Rennie blinked unbelievingly. Blond hair, light blue eyes, an intensely alert expression. Quite unmistakably the ghost girl she had seen at Silver Springs! Dev Deveraux's friend, Isobel Sandison. What could it mean? Maybe she should see a psychiatrist. . . . She managed to acknowledge the introductions, feeling herself alien and conspicuous in her torn shirt, her jeans that were covered with red dust, and was thankful to have attention diverted from her by the sound of the Cessna's engine.

"I'd better get moving and drive out to the airstrip," said Dev. "Want to come, Isobel?"

"I'd love to," the blond girl said animatedly. Her accent was Australian, and in addition, more than somewhat affected. Rennie thought instinctively as the other girl walked past her without a glance, *She doesn't like mixing with cooks.* She watched as Dev followed Isobel out into the midday sunlight.

"Isobel's forgotten her hat," murmured her aunt.

Dr. Grace said frowningly, "You gave us all heart

failure, Rennald, with your antics in the sky. We couldn't think who Tim had got hold of. What on earth possessed you?''

Rennie sat down on one end of a couch whose springs were definitely not what they had been, and whose upholstery was nearing the end of its life. She felt unsteady despite the brandy—the shock of meeting Isobel had been distinctly unnerving. She told Dr. Grace wearily, "I've done a lot of parachuting. I just had an uncontrollable urge to jump again. I'm sorry."

"So you should be. And despite this idea of Dev's that you should stay here and work, you can go back with Tim and Nancy after lunch." She crossed her large nylon-clad legs and looked at her snakeskin shoes. "I told you I didn't want you here."

Rennie's eyes widened. "I understood you'd changed your mind. Tim said you asked for me to come—"

"If anyone asked you to come, it was my nephew," said Grace coldly. "Certainly I didn't."

Nina Sandison's round face wore a pained expression as she listened. She was a fastidious-looking little woman, with her careful makeup and her neatly waved light red hair. Everything about her looked neat and natty, in fact, but clearly she was finding the heat trying, and Rennie thought that she was certainly unused to living under conditions such as those that existed at Nimmitibel. For her own part, she was well aware that the homestead was old, shabby, its furniture—what there was of it—battered, its curtains and the few floor rugs faded and worn, its kitchen a monstrous furnace. But she couldn't see that Dev was living in the rough. A woman, she reflected, could soon have made the place very much more attractive and comfortable. First a thorough spring-cleaning, bowls of flowers, then new curtains, new upholstery—maybe a few new pieces of furniture. The windows were wonderful, and the scenery outside was dramatic rather than monotonous, far more exciting than that at Silver Springs. The colors were fantastic and so clear that perspective became something completely new. Even the far horizon looked oddly close. She imagined that sunset over that red earth would be really something. And the birds which she had seen from the air would be coming down to the water. Isobel had probably assessed it already in rather the same way, but Dr. Grace wouldn't want Isobel to look on the bright side. She wanted one thing only, and that was to shift Dev over to Silver Springs.

"I would welcome a new cook," said Nina Sandison, opening wide round eyes that were light blue like those of her niece but not nearly so intense in their expression. "The food we are served by that aboriginal woman Ettie—fond of her though Mr. Deveraux undoubtedly is—is quite indescribable. There are vegetables in the garden—tomatoes, carrots, I've even seen lettuce—one could make a salad. But it's always a hot meal, and servings big enough to fatten a dozen Christmas geese." She shuddered, and Rennie smiled, but Dr. Grace gave a shrug.

"That's Nimmitibel. No good cook would ever stay here. Old Ettie out there has been cooking for the stockmen since she was a teenager, and Dev simply couldn't care less. He'll be as bad as that head stockman of his if he stays out here much longer. As it is he spends half his time sleeping under the stars at the muster camps. He's only come in to the homestead because he has guests."

"It sounds romantic," said Nina Sandison doubtfully.

"It can sound very romantic when you're not living here," agreed Grace. "There's nothing like experiencing it to teach you how far from romantic it really is." She sent Rennie an indifferent glance. "You'll be missing nothing, Rennald, if you go back this afternoon. On the contrary, in fact.''

Rennie could see her idea very very plainly. Isobel was going to have it hard. She was going to see things exactly as they were, and she was going to think of Silver Springs with longing. In fact, Grace planned to use her to maneuver Dev back onto the family property. For some reason Rennie didn't like this idea at all. Not, she told herself as she leaned back on the couch and closed her eyes, that she cared one bit where Dev and Isobel Sandison lived. It was the Langs she was thinking of—she didn't want to see them tossed out of their home, just to please Dr. Grace. Isobel could learn to live at Nimmitibel. *I would learn,* thought Rennie, and just now, with her eyes closed and no one picking on her, she didn't think it would be all that hard. But she wasn't, she simply *was not,* going to be used by Dr. Grace to further her own selfish schemes. No matter what her employer wanted, somehow or other she was going to stay here and make things as pleasant as she could—give Isobel an unobtrusive lead. And just as a side issue, she would show Dev Deveraux what she was made of. By now, she had completely rid herself of the illusion that he wanted to play games with her, but she wondered fleetingly why he had told her to forget about his head stockman—a quite unnecessary warning, for she wasn't likely to be tangling with that tough character.

But sleeping under the stars—

Maybe the brandy had made her drowsy. She was roused by the sound of voices and the realization that it was time for lunch.

"I watched you going down, Rennie," Nancy said as they went into the dining room where their places were carelessly laid on a white linen cloth that needed ironing and had not been starched. Tim and Dev appeared from

the office where they had been having a conference—
discussing the northeast paddock, not her, Rennie hoped.
"I quite envied you when I saw you floating around
under your big parachute. And then you played catch-as-
catch-can with that twister. I thought it would fizzle out
before it caught up with you. What did you do to your
arm?"

"Scratched it," said Rennie with a shrug. "It's
nothing."

She noticed that Tim looked chastened, guessed that
he had been given a dressing down over what had
happened and determined to apologize to him as soon as
lunch was over. She wanted to know too if there was to be
any retribution—and if there was, she would kick up the
most tremendous fuss.

Dinner was steak with sodden dumplings and potatoes
baked in their skins, homemade bread that was good and
an unimaginative but adequate desert of tinned peaches
and yellow custard. Not at all the ideal meal to make in
the middle of a very hot day. Or, to be honest, at any time
at all. Nina Sandison looked faint, Dr. Grace scarcely
touched her food, nor did Isobel. Nancy made a joke of it
and demolished the lot, and Tim and the boss did the
same, though they dispensed with the joking. Rennie did
her best and wondered how on earth she was going to
cope with that oven of a kitchen and that huge and
terrifying-looking black stove. It was not the cheeriest of
prospects.

She waylaid Tim afterward on the way out of the
dining room, said her piece and discovered that no
action had been taken against him, which was a relief.
On the veranda, Dev said, "I'll fly you and Nancy back
when you're ready, Tim. Do you want to come along,
Isobel?"

Isobel grimaced and shuddered. "Not in that little plane, thank you."

"You'd better take Rennald back," said Dr. Grace. "And her luggage, too," she added in case Dev thought she meant merely for the ride.

He raised his eyebrows. "I didn't know you'd adjusted to Etta's meals, Grace. Surely your cook can please you better than that."

Dr. Grace didn't answer that suggestion. "For goodness' sake, why would the poor girl want to stay here?" She turned to Rennie. "Your luggage is in the front hall. You'd better fetch it."

Rennie hesitated, but what could she do? There seemed nothing for it but to resign herself to going back with Nancy and Tim. But she was not going to hang around at Silver Springs. She would get to Adelaide somehow—get out of their hair, forget these people and their tangled affairs. She went into the hall, picked up her suitcases one in each hand, and found Dev had followed her.

"So you're going."

"What else would you expect me to do?" she flared. "I thought Dr. Warren wanted me here. She doesn't. So I'll go. I'm not in a position to pick and choose."

His blue eyes looked her over sardonically. "You won't even put up a fight," he mocked. "Could it be that the sight of my kitchen has scared you off? Or the rough, tough face of the land you claimed you were so interested in? Odd, that timidity of yours—when one remembers the tricks you got up to this morning."

She felt her color rise. "That has nothing to do with it! But I happen to dislike hanging around where I'm not wanted."

"But you *are* wanted, Rennald Baxter," he said blandly. "You must have seen that for yourself at the dinner table today. We need a good cook. If you really want to stay, there's work to be done. It's up to you."

She thought about that. She did want to stay—because of Tim and Meg Lang. She had had all that out with herself earlier on. And as well, she was interested in seeing Nimmitibel. . . . She set down her bags.

"Are you offering me a job? I assure you, your kitchen won't deter me," she added dryly, hoping she would somehow be able to prove the truth of that if necessary.

"No?" He looked a little amused. "Well, that's fine. . . . But a job—no. I don't think I want to offer you a job. That way, Grace might find grounds for quarreling with me. Let's put it like this—you please the ladies at meal times, and in between you may do as you like."

"Fair enough," said Rennie. "But," she added, "I don't think it will work. Your aunt wants me to go."

He narrowed his eyes. "I think we can be diplomatic about that. Suppose I tell her—threaten her, if you like— that if you go now, you go out of her life for good?"

Rennie smiled a little. It might not work. She knew why Dr. Grace didn't want her here, though it appeared that Dev didn't. "Very well. If you can engineer it—I would like to . . . to see the country."

"Leave it to me," he said confidently, and for some reason he appeared immensely pleased with himself. He picked up her luggage. "I'll take this along to the bedroom you'll be sleeping in. And by the way," he paused to say, "that great kitchen I took you through this morning is Etta's domain— that's a kitchen of a size for cooking meals for hungry stockmen when they're in from the mustering camps. We do have another kitchen, and though it hasn't seen much use, you'll find it's well equipped, I think."

Rennie breathed a sigh of relief.

After that, she went out with the others in the car to the

hangar. She took Dev's parachute pack with her, and he left her there while he flew Nancy and Tim back to Silver Springs. She had not quite finished her repacking when he came back. It was extremely hot in the hangar, and she hadn't yet changed out of her dirty clothes—what was the point, until she could shower and feel civilized again? She wondered if she had done a silly thing in being persuaded to stay on here. Persuaded? Wasn't it what she had wanted herself? It was, and yet she felt uneasily that Dev had manipulated her—got his own way.

She was afraid of Dev Deveraux. She was beginning to realize to the full that he was a man with a great deal of charm attached to his hardness. And that he belonged—or almost belonged—to another woman.

When he had brought the Cessna down, he came straight into the hangar. He wore a white shirt with an open neck and light colored cotton trousers, and those fantastically blue eyes in the monochrome face with its flash of white teeth unsteadied her.

She looked up at him briefly and said in a businesslike way, "I haven't damaged your 'chute, but I won't take any credit for that. It was sheer good luck. Will you use it again?"

He shrugged. "I don't think so. I've finished with that phase of my life."

She didn't ask him why. She was winding the bridle cord into a figure eight on top of the canopy that was now stowed away in its sleeve, and she gave it all her attention.

Neither of them spoke until the packing was completed, and then he said, "I'll admit you made a very efficient job of that, Rennald Baxter."

She looked up and met the blueness of his gaze. It was dim at this end of the hangar in contrast with the brilliant blaze of light by the doors. The very air seemed to throb with heat and she was thinking longingly of a shower in that big white bathroom at the homestead when she became aware that his glance had settled on her right cheek, with its small star-shaped scar.

"Another trophy from your jumping exploits?" he asked.

This time she didn't pretend not to understand. She said a casual, "That's right," and felt her color rise annoyingly.

"It couldn't have been a whirlwind in the fresh green fields of England," he said consideringly. "So what was it? A bad landing? Didn't you have a good instructor?"

"I had a very good instructor," she retorted, and she thought of Pete, and of the hurt he had inflicted. Surprisingly, it took an effort.

"Then what?"

Her lips twisted wryly. She could tell the truth and he wouldn't believe a word of it, so why not? At least he wouldn't ask her again.

"I lost my cool. I met up with a ghost."

He didn't laugh. He didn't even look particularly surprised. But he did look interested. "I see. Up in the air?"

"Yes ... floating along beside me ... just for a second. But I'm not sure whether or not she had her chute with her."

"Someone you knew?"

"Not really. I'd just met her before take-off."

He looked thoughtful and offered her a cigarette. She took it and let him light it for her, then watched him light his own.

"She'd done some parachuting, of course, and had given it up," he said then.

Rennie's eyes widened. "How would you know?" She was amazed that he was taking her so seriously, that he hadn't laughed her off the face of the earth—or said that she ought to be certified.

"It's logical," he said. He leaned comfortably back against the wall and surveyed her lazily. "Ghosts don't inhabit places they've never visited. At a guess, I'd say your ghost girl wanted to be up there again."

Well, perhaps Susie Rainer had wanted to be up there again. Rennie didn't know very much about her—except that she meant a great deal more to Pete Morgan than Rennie had ever meant—

She asked carelessly, "Do you really take ghosts seriously, Mr. Deveraux? Or are you making fun of me?"

"I'm not making fun of you. I'm interested. In my view, there's nothing particularly mysterious about the usual ghost. The point of interest lies in the person who sees such things. I believe I told you earlier that I had a great deal to do with the aboriginals around Silver Springs when I was an impressionable child. I grew accustomed to taking for granted psychic powers—skills—that the average person in our so-called civilized world would think impossible. The passing on of information, emotions, over long distances—a sort of pre-speech form of communication—"

Rennie said frowningly as he paused, "What's that got to do with apparitions?"

"How can I explain it? Let's just say that a ghost is . . . a telepathic projection of an image, picked up by someone who happens to be on the same wave length . . . or, in other words, is sensitive to such psychic vibrations. In this case you've told me about, I'd say this girl you saw had often skydived over that particular field, possibly was a pupil of your jumping instructor. That she'd enjoyed the sport and on this occasion was doing a bit of wishful thinking. And you . . . caught her at it, as it were."

"I see," said Rennie slowly. It seemed a reasonable enough explanation. Yet she was not thinking of Susie Rainer now. She was thinking of Isobel Sandison in the sitting room at Silver Springs. Perhaps she had just arrived at Nimmitibel and was wishing herself back in the homestead where she had first met Dev. Would she be in league with Grace Warren to get Dev out of Nimmitibel? And would he send Tim Lang away and go?

It's going to be a battle, thought Rennie. She looked at Dev speculatively and was taken aback when he asked her with a sudden change of direction, almost as if he had read her thoughts, "By the way, where have you met Isobel Sandison before?"

Color rushed guiltily to her cheeks. She said quickly, "Nowhere. Why?"

"I saw your face when you met her—you did a kind of double take. You're sure?"

"Of course." She looked around her wildly. "Where does this gear go?"

"Give it to me."

She watched him stow it away in a locker and drew nervously on her cigarette.

"I'd have sworn," he said thoughtfully, "that you'd encountered her somewhere. However—" unexpectedly he rested his hand lightly on her shoulder and shepherded her out of the hangar "—she's an Adelaide girl—works on a newspaper." He named it, looking down at her questioningly. Rennie felt too conscious of that hand laid in such easy friendliness upon her shoulder. It unbalanced her.

She said, "I didn't meet anyone socially in Adelaide. I'm a . . . a cook—"

"Even cooks must live and love and amuse themselves," he said. "I promise I won't forget that while you're here."

She felt herself flinch, and drew away from his touch. *Don't try to sweep me off my feet,* she warned him silently, and aloud she said, "Don't worry, I'll find ways of amusing myself, Mr. Deveraux."

"I'll supervise it," he said smoothly. "That's part of my job here—to keep an eye on everything."

CHAPTER FOUR

STARTING THE NEXT DAY, Rennie set about making the
homestead at Nimmitibel more attractive.

For Isobel.

In the mornings, Dev was not around. He couldn't
keep an eye on every part of his station at once, no matter
what he liked to think, and he spent mornings with his
cattle and his men. The afternoons and evenings—and
this was something new, judging by earlier remarks of
Grace's—he came back home. There, he kept an eye on
his guests. He entertained them, in Isobel's case, or
argued with them, in Grace's. As for Nina—she was
rarely available in the afternoons. After lunch she relaxed—or collapsed—in her room, and once she was
conscious again, she seemed to prefer to study Dev from
a little distance. Rennie thought she was the type of
woman who could live very well in a cosy comfortable
feminine world, and that she had little use or time for
men. It might be a good way to be. . . .

For Rennie, the mornings, once breakfast was over,
were hers to do what she liked with, and she put in her
time making improvements, first in the running of the
household, instructing the two young aboriginals who
did the housework, and tutoring the old fellow who
tended the vegetable garden as to what fresh vegetables
she would like each day. The homestead needed a thorough doing out. All its cracks and corners were filled with

red dust, the curtains needed washing and the windows cleaning. The silverware hadn't been polished in a long time, and there were good glasses and bits of china hidden away at the backs of cupboards that could be used. Table linen too.

It would be a lengthy process, but even if she could not see it through, she could still get it under way and give Isobel a start. At first she had to threaten and bully Iris and Cilly, but soon she had them working good-humoredly—as long as they knew she was around to check up on them. After the first day, they brought two more "girls" over from the aboriginal quarters—Cilly's mother and her very young aunt—and quite a lot of cleaning up and laundering was accomplished. Rennie wished that she could have papered the dark walls or painted them, and that she could have had a free hand with the soft furnishings. She'd have used clear soft colors that would give the drabness of the rooms a lift. However, something must be left for Isobel, and in the meantime it was a help to fill the vases with flowers—long training stems of bougainvillea, pink and white olean-ders, big white daisies with papery petals. The oleanders soon wilted and drooped, but while they lasted they were pretty and there were plenty of them on the trees shading the side paths.

She was in the garden cutting bougainvilleas one morning when Nina Sandison, wearing a wide-brimmed straw hat she had got from the station store, joined her.

"Oh, this interminable heat!" she complained. "Peo-ple say it's dry and therefore tolerable, but I'm afraid it's too much for me. I often wish that Isobel had asked one of her young friends to accompany her here, rather than her old aunt. And now, with you and Dr. Warren here, she doesn't even need me for a chaperone. I would dearly love to sneak away, but it would be rather in the nature of a major operation, don't you agree?''

Rennie agreed wholeheartedly. It would be no piece of cake to sneak off from a place sitting out in the middle of miles and miles of hot red sand.

"I don't know why," said Aunt Nina, following her along the shady path, "my niece had to fall in love with someone living in this part of the world." Her pale blue eyes were sad and wistful. "Adelaide is so lovely. Of course, the summers are hot, but one has air-conditioning, all the comforts. And there are a number of nice men there she could have chosen—her own boss, for one, who although he is some years older than Mr. Deveraux, would give her anything she asked for. But she has to choose . . . this." She gestured toward the burning sky, the shimmer of the mulga-dotted red earth beyond the garden. "These articles she is writing are a mere excuse for being here. In my view, one could say all there is to be said about the Outback in a single page. However, Isobel is a practical girl in many ways, and it was wise for her to come to Nimmitibel to see how she likes it. Yet now it seems to me she has completely lost her head—she sees nothing but Mr. Deveraux."

She sighed regretfully and looked at Rennie as if for comfort and reassurance of some kind. "I believe it's very much more pleasant at Silver Springs—each bedroom with its own bathroom, the furniture comfortable, the garden green—"

Rennie glanced over the stems she had cut with their cubistic lanternlike purple red flowers. She said cheerfully, "Oh, I'm sure this homestead could be made just as agreeable with a little effort. And it's fun to do the decorating oneself. I don't really think that there's all that much difference between the two places."

Aunt Nina's face fell a little. "Oh dear. I'll be glad

when it's all settled and I can go home to my nice little flat and my friends in the city.''

I shall be glad too, thought Rennie, but somehow she didn't feel particularly cheerful just then. As she arranged the flowers later she thought about what Aunt Nina had told her so guilelessly. So Isobel was writing articles about the Outback and seeing how she liked it at the same time. How *does* she like it, Rennie wondered. It was not easy to imagine the trim efficient intelligent Isobel Sandison settling down here. But then Dev Deveraux must surely be something of an inducement, and she had apparently completely lost her usually level head over him.

Rennie shut off her thoughts deliberately, took the flowers inside, then went out to the kitchen garden. There, she managed to persuade old Lernem to part with a couple of young lettuce and some small sweet carrots. She had set some cold chicken in aspic jelly the night before, and she was going to make a simple French dressing for the salad. In her mind's eye she could see the pretty dish she would present for lunch—set out on the yellow and white spotted cloth at the end of the side veranda.

She jumped when Dr. Grace appeared in the neat little kitchen that had scarcely been used, if ever, to say complainingly, "Really, Rennald, I wonder what all this effort of yours is in aid of. I'm not paying you to impress Isobel Sandison with the possibilities of the Nimmitibel homestead.''

Rennie colored faintly. "Still—there are possibilities.''

"So limited that they could keep an intelligent girl happy no longer than a month. Unless you subscribe to the old-fashioned view that a woman in love will put up with anything for her man. . . . At all events, stick to what you're paid to do in future, please—and that's the cooking."

Rennie said nothing. She wasn't sure whether Dr. Grace was paying her or not. Whether, in fact, she was working for Dev Deveraux or his aunt. At some point she would have to find out, but just now she wasn't worrying. The house was going to be kept clean, and Isobel and Aunt Nina were going to have fresh towels and smooth bed linen, a shining bathroom and cool drinks whenever they wanted them. As well as pretty dressed-up salads for lunch.

Dev, she was certain, noticed nothing. Except the salads.

"You're right—she can cook," he said to Grace over lunch that day, just as though Rennie were not at the table too. He added, "I never thought I'd be sitting down at a ladies' luncheon party on Nimmitibel. Where would you get a salad like this in Adelaide, Isobel?"

Isobel named a restaurant instantly, one that Rennie did not know, of course, and Dev crumbled a piece of bread and remarked, "I must go there sometime. Meanwhile, there's no need." He looked over at Rennie. "Make dinner somewhat more substantial, will you? I'm not accustomed to eating like a bird."

"Birds," said Aunt Nina, "eat a surprisingly large amount. I've been reading one of your books, Mr. Deveraux, and a galah will eat—oh, I forget how many thousands of grass seeds in a day."

"Touché, Miss Sandison," said Dev. He pushed back his chair. "Who's for a drive out to the water hole and a swim later on in the afternoon? Isobel? You'll see the birds coming down to drink—including Miss Sandison's galahs—and if you like, we can boil the billy and make tea in traditional bush style."

"Lovely," said Isobel.

"Bring your notebook along," said Dev. He glanced at Rennie and raised his eyebrows questioningly. Was he asking her to come along, too? She would have liked to go. But to jump up and follow him when he so much as raised his eyebrows—that was a little too eager.

"I won't be going," she said. "I've the dinner to think of."

"Of course. My dinner. You're quite the little housewife, aren't you?" he mocked.

"Cook," she corrected him levelly, but she flushed all the same.

He gave her a hard look. "Maybe you'd better not swim with that arm yet, anyhow. I'll take a look at it this evening."

"Thank you," she said politely. "But it's healing up perfectly. I've been looking after it."

She got up from the table and carried some of the dishes out to the kitchen, and Isobel followed her with the teapot. She put it down on the counter top and looked around her. She had smiled her approval of the salad earlier on, but she had said nothing. In fact, she had never bothered to say much at all to Rennie. They were not, her attitude seemed to apply, on the same footing here.

Now she said almost chattily, "It's a sweet little kitchen, isn't it?"

"And easy to work in," said Rennie agreeably.

Isobel smiled at her. But even when she smiled, Rennie could see a hardness, a calculating look, at the back of her rather fine intelligent eyes. "That's splendid. You must appreciate it after having been more or less dragged out here on a job. I did rather admire you for arriving with such dash. We were all quite stunned. That really *was* an entrance. I'm sure my—I'm sure Dev was quite knocked out to see the cook coming down by parachute."

Rennie began to stack the dishes in the sink. Isobel had almost said "my fiancé" and that was revealing. She had also more or less accused Rennie of deliberately trying to impress Dev. Uneasily, she was aware that she had, in a way, done that jump to make an impression, but not of the sort that Isobel had implied. Mostly, she had jumped for her own satisfaction. But as well, she had wanted to show Dev that she was not a hothouse plant, not overly sheltered, not timid.

She said cautiously, "I suppose you thought I was showing off. It's hard to explain, but I get a tremendous kick out of jumping, and it was too much of a temptation when the chance came up."

"It seems a senseless sort of pastime to me," said Isobel. "Personally, I value my whole and healthy body too much to be interested. How is your arm, by the way?"

"It's perfectly all right. It was just a scratch."

"I'm so glad," said Isobel. "I'll tel Dev not to bother looking at it. Well, I must be off to enjoy an afternoon in this marvelously exciting country. I'll see you later."

Rennie was thoughtful. So Isobel liked this part of the country. She must have settled down since the day she had arrived and sent her thoughts over to the comfort and beauty of Silver Springs. Perhaps it was not really so surprising. She seemed a sophisticated sort of girl, yet, come to think of it, while she was smart she was not too smart. Her makeup, while skilful, was moderate, her clothes were up-to-the-minute but more feminine than anything else. Femininity without fussiness. That summed Isobel up in a way. She was a girl who was very sure of herself. She wasn't impulsive or undecided, and there was just a hint of hardness at the back of her light blue eyes that suggested to Rennie that somehow Isobel would look after herself. *If she likes it here,* thought Rennie, drying the dishes that she had been washing automatically, *she will stay. It won't matter what Dr. Grace says, or what I do, either. The only person who will really count will be Dev.* She wished a little forlornly that she had gone when she had had the chance and not succumbed to Dev's trickery. Why had she? When he was so patently using her?

She didn't try to answer her own question. She put away the dishes and looked around blankly for a minute or two. She ought to think about that substantial dinner. She ought to prepare some sort of a dessert, put it to cool in the fridge. She had boasted to Dev that she was the cook, and that was exactly what she was. Yet now she wished she had taken up his implied invitation to go with him and Isobel to the water hole, instead of being so suspicious and staying here to think about food—to what purpose?

On an impulse, she went to her room and found her swimsuit, a one-piece affair of aquamarine that matched her eyes. She undressed and stepped into it, covered it with a button-up skirt of emerald green cotton and pulled a blue shirt over her head. She took a towel and a hat and slipped on canvas shoes. Where was this water hole they talked about? They were going to drive there— so she wasn't going to try to walk. Aunt Nina was stretched out asleep on an old cane lounge chair on the veranda, and Dr. Grace, spectacles on the end of her nose, sat in a chair farther along. She was smartly dressed as usual and apparently unbothered by the heat, and the book she was reading looked as if it weighed about ten pounds. Its pages of solid print were embellished by photographs of noble-looking bulls—champions, without a doubt—so Rennie concluded that the book was probably about cattle breeding. No use asking her where the water hole was. She decided to ask Cilly

instead, and presently was directed toward the big
lagoon.

"Little bit water alongside big water under myalls.
D wn along the track there, Rennie."

Rennie took a bicycle she had seen in one of the
garages and rode over the bumpy red track. Away to her
left, a stretch of saltbush glittered silver in strange and
beautiful contrast to the bare red earth around, and away
on the horizon the usual water mirages shimmered. She
could see it all etched on her mind's eye even when she
looked away and she thought it would be there for ever.
Once she reached the banks of the lagoon there was
shade, a lovely light feathery shade that flicked over her
in splinters as she pedaled slowly along. The water
looked more green than blue down here by the trees, and
half a dozen colored parrots like the one she had seen in
the sky flew out of the mulgas with harsh cries as she
passed by. Otherwise there was an almost eerie silence
and not a sign of cattle anywhere. The lagoon glittered
still and glassy under the burning sun.

Presently she reached a thick grove of trees of a
different kind—myalls, she guessed—and here the water
branched off into a side channel. She got off her bicycle
and leaving it propped against a tree in the shade,
walked slowly along beneath the trees. Still she could
hear nothing. Perhaps Isobel and Dev hadn't started on
their swim yet—perhaps they thought it too soon after
lunch. She hoped she was not going to stumble on a love
scene, and the thought almost made her turn back. But
the stillness was almost absolute—lizards rustled in the
leaves, that was all—and here the water was like a dark
mirror, crowded thickly around with trees, and somehow, she thought, not the most attractive place for a
swim. Farther ahead, it snaked to the left and sunlight
burst through the trees, and presently she found a small

and perfect pool with long sloping banks of coarse pinkish sand.

The swimming hole for sure, but no Dev and Isobel.

She felt both frustrated and relieved, but after a moment she pulled off her blouse, unbuttoned her skirt, discarded shoes and hat and made her way down the sun-hot sand. The water deepened swiftly a couple of feet from the edge and was warm enough to feel like the softest of embraces. It received her so gently that she scarcely felt she was in a different element.

She swam slowly, sometimes with her head under water and her eyes open, so she could see to the bottom of this deep water hole with its smooth red sand, red and white and purple rocks and occasional crayfish. She had turned on her back when she heard a whistle. She thought it was a bird at first, but the whistling turned into a human voice, and she turned on her front and listened in astonishment.

"Wrap me up with my stockwhip and bluey
    And bury me deep down below,
    Where the dingoes and crows can't molest me.
    In the shade where the coolibahs grow."

Mournful words, yet they were sung with a kind of cheerful inconsequence. Rennie searched along the bank and in a moment she discovered Jake Ridley not far from where she had left her clothes, his back against a tree. She swam toward the bank and came out on the sand.

He despised women, but she didn't care; in fact, if anything, it suited her very well—she needn't be on her guard with a man like that.

He watched her as she left the water. He wore the same dusty-looking clothes he had worn before, and once again she was stunned by his extravagantly good looks, by those brilliant yellow green eyes, emphasized by the added attraction of unruly jet black hair, revealed when he removed his hat.

"Hello!" he greeted her abruptly.

"Hello," said Rennie. She continued to walk toward him, or rather toward her pile of clothes and the towel that was lying on top of them. His eyes were intent on discovering everything they could about her with such complete frankness that it was decidedly ill-mannered. But she stooped for her towel unhurriedly and draped it casually around her, then pushed back her streaming hair. In other circumstances, she would have toweled her hair first, but this time it would have to wait. And perhaps she had been just a little wrong in imagining she need not be on her guard. . . .

She said in mockery of what he had said to her the other day, "So it's a human being! I thought at first it was a bird whistling. What are you doing here?"

He laughed briefly, with a curious mirthlessness.

"I've been looking for you," he said. "I thought I'd see if you were still on Nimmitibel=where the civilization is—or if Dev had sent you away with a flea in your ear. One of the lubras said you'd come down to take a swim, so here I am. How's your arm? Did you get it stitched up?"

She shook her head. "There was no need. Mr. Deveraux pulled the edges together and fixed them with a bandage, and it's pretty well as good as new, I think. You didn't happen to run into him and Isobel Sandison on your way over, I suppose?" The water from her dripping hair was running down her face, and she tossed her head back with a quick movement. She would dearly have liked to take the towel to it, but Jake's eyes were roving over her long legs, and she hadn't the courage to expose any more of her skin to his scrutiny.

"I didn't see a soul," he told her.

Rennie thought she felt relieved. She didn't want to look as though she were chasing Dev, and besides, he had told her to forget about his head stockman, and she somehow thought he had really meant it. It would be preferable not to linger here with Jake—just in case Dev and Isobel should turn up. Besides, she definitely didn't feel all that safe, one way or another. She said with slight diffidence, "Well, thank you for coming to inquire about me. It was very nice of you." She couldn't quite bring herself to say his name, perhaps because it would put them on a more friendly footing than she wanted. It was a rather ridiculous way to look at it, because out here Christian names were the rule rather than the exception. True, Dev always called Nina, "Miss Sandison," but it was certainly not for the same reason that made her unable to call this man Jake—or any name at all. "I must get back to the homestead now, to see about dinner."

With one foot she began to separate her canvas shoes from her small heap of clothing. Surely he would take the hint and go away and leave her to dress.

But he didn't.

"Don't go yet," he said. "Where's the hurry?" His strange green eyes flickered over her face and the whiteness of her neck, her slim hands that were holding the towel across her breast. "I didn't come over just to ask about your arm. I wanted to see you again. You're the first woman I've met in a long time who hasn't turned my stomach."

The phrase made Rennie blink. It was a doubtful sort of compliment and one she didn't welcome. And yet despite this man's abruptness and his rudeness, somehow she couldn't altogether dislike him. She smiled wryly and said, "Thank you for the compliment, Mr.—"

"Come on, call me Jake," he said.

She swallowed nervously. "Jake," she repeated reluctantly "But I really do have to get back. So if you don't mind, I'd like to get my clothes on—"

"Go ahead! I'll turn my back at the strategic moment. You have only to say the word. At least you can stop clutching that towel around you. There's nothing much wrong with your figure, except maybe you're a little bit thin."

Rennie grimaced inwardly. In silence she turned to her heap of clothes, stood with her back to him, tossed down her towel and quickly pulled her shirt over her head. Then she wrapped the green skirt around her waist, buttoned it up, regretted the fact that it was going to get wet and slipped on her shoes. Behind her he whistled that tune again. She asked, partly to hide a feeling of embarrassment as she turned around to face him, "What's that you're always whistling?"

"Am I?" He looked vaguely surprised. "Must be 'The Dying Stockman,' " he said after considering for a moment. "Yes, that's what it is. Must be my signature tune." Casually, he put a hard suntanned hand on Rennie's waist as they walked along the track under the trees, and she knew with a feeling of dread that he was going to try to kiss her before they reached her bicycle. Well, it was not going to happen. She was fussy about who she kissed, and even the men whose kisses she had wanted Jean-Yves and Peter Morgan—had turned out to be unworthy of love and trust. But this man here in the emptiness of the bush—how was she to contend with him? There just mustn't be an opportunity for him to kiss her.

She began to move quickly ahead of him, to run in fact, but then she stopped in case such haste caused him to make a grab at her. She was certain those darkly-tanned, muscly-looking arms of his would be too strong for her to escape. She had slowed down when she tripped over a root, and before she knew it she was floundering in the water—that dark-looking water where the trees leaned down so close—and its unexpected coldness gave her a distinct shock. She surfaced and caught out blindly at the hands that reached down for her, and in two seconds she had been pulled up onto the bank, her back was against a tree trunk, and Jake Ridley's mouth was on hers.

She gasped and struggled hard to free herself—

Footsteps sounded, and Jake took his lips from hers so he could look around and see who was coming. Rennie looked over his shoulder and she saw, too. It was Dev Deveraux, of course, and behind him, with a look of distaste on her face, Isobel Sandison, trim in blue denim shirt and jeans.

Rennie said absurdly, "Please let me get by." Please let me get by! Wasn't that the laugh of the year? But of course Jake did let her get by, and crimson-cheeked she continued along the path toward Dev. Her eyes, sea-blue and bright, looked straight at him and dared him to say anything. Hadn't the cook the right to go swimming fully clad—and to be kissed by the head stockman if that was the way they both wanted it? And now was not the time to tell him that she didn't want it—

"I thought I told you to keep out of the water with that arm," he said, one hand shooting out to grab her as she attempted to edge past him.

"It slipped my mind," said Rennie. Her face was white now. He had warned her to keep away from the stockman, too, and it wouldn't look as though she had remembered that, either.

Jake said placatingly, "She slipped and fell in the water and I helped her out, boss—and lost my head for a moment. She's far too pretty and smart a girl for a station cook."

Rennie closed her eyes. This was a miniature nightmare.

"Miss Baxter is not the station cook." Dev's voice was clipped. "She is my guest. And I don't want to see you loafing around here, Jake, when there's a muster on. I left you in charge, remember? Was there anything in particular you wanted from the homestead –or me?"

"No. I just took time off to see how the–how your *guest* is after her little tumble the other day. She was on my mind."

"She needn't be. She's being adequately cared for, I assure you."

Jake was then ignored, and Rennie thought, *Dev doesn't like him much. They're not what you would call mates.*

Isobel, she discovered, had tactfully gone back a few yards along the path and was looking up into the trees with a thoughtful and interested air. She asked casually as Dev, still gripping Rennie hard, caught up with her, "Would those be mulga parrots, Dev? So bright, and wearing little dabs of yellow feathers on their ears."

"Yes, they're mulga parrots, Isobel," said Dev. "I don't know what sort of a story you can write about them, though."

"None," she said, with her intelligent smile. "They're hardly exciting–I was just interested."

In mulga parrots, but not in the sordid little affairs of the cook and the head stockman. Had she heard Dev call her his guest, Rennie wondered. Or was she so genuinely uninterested that she had not bothered listening?

Dev put the bicycle in the back of the Land Rover and the dripping Rennie in beside it. "Sorry, Isobel—we'll have our swim another day. I'll have to put a new dressing on this girl's arm.''

Rennie was sure that was unnecessary. She was a healthy girl and her arm was nearly better. He just wanted to make the point that she had disobeyed his instructions.

At least he let her change out of her wet clothes before he attended to her arm. The wound was clean and it was mending nicely. He swabbed it with antiseptic, renewed the protective covering and the bandage, and commented, "Well, fortunately your system's dealing adequately with that." Then, just when she thought she was to be allowed to go, he shot out, "Now I want the full story of what went on out there."

"Nothing," said Rennie. "And if you hadn't come along it would still have been nothing."

"No? You were as jam packed with fright as a honeybee is with nectar. And it wasn't because I interrupted the scene. Jake Ridley doesn't hold women sacred, though as a rule he steers clear of them—that's one reason he's working in the Outback. But I warned you once before not to try your charms on him. If men don't fascinate you—I think that was your phrase—why don't you leave them alone?" His blue eyes regarded her almost savagely. "Do you just want to . . . find out? Or do you perversely relish the passion you arouse?"

Rennie listened to his tirade and found she was having trouble keeping back tears—angry tears, hurt tears. She *had* been frightened. He was right about that. But not about anything else. She hadn't tried her charms on Jake Ridley. She didn't want to "find out," as he had put it. Nor had she relished Jake Ridley's passion—far from it. She said, trying to keep her voice steady, "All right—so it looked bad to you. But it was only because I fell in the water that he touched me. And anyhow," she added illogically but with feeling, "one would think you ought to be able to trust your own stockmen."

He laughed incredulously. "Now come on—surely neither of us is so naïve as to deny that the mating instinct of the human male is a strong one, even in a man who has exiled himself from civilized society." He frowned and his blue eyes looked at her reflectively. "Yet on second thoughts, I don't know about you. Maybe you're a girl who has her head in the clouds in more ways than one. You never talk about yourself, do you? What have you left behind in England? A broken home—divorced parents?"

"Good heavens," said Rennie, trying bewilderedly to follow his train of thought, "of course not. My parents aren't living now, but they were very happy together, I assure you. And I have three older sisters, each of whom is very satisfactorily married, if it's of any interest to you."

He leaned against the wall—they were, rather incongruously, still in the big bathroom, shining now, since Rennie had taken over—and surveyed her as if she were some sort of curiosity. "Then why the problems? What sort of—God knows, innocent—love affair has given you your kinky outlook?"

He paused. She said nothing. What did he want? Confessions? He wasn't going to get them. He would think she was a very gullible girl if he knew what a hopeless love life hers had been.

"Well?" he prompted.

"You know all that's necessary about me," she said coolly. "I can cook, and I like parachuting. Isn't that enough?"

"It seems it will have to be. I can't force you to tell me what you don't want me to know. I won't ask questions, but I'll say just one more thing. And I want you to keep it very firmly fixed right at the front of that unfathomable mind of yours." There was a harshness in his voice, and she waited for him to go on. "Out here we don't see all that many attractive young women. A girl like you can be a big temptation, especially to a hungry man who's been given a bit of encouragement. If you don't remember that, you might find you really have problems."

"You advise me to stay safely in the kitchen, do you, Mr. Deveraux?" she retorted, though she had reddened angrily at his suggestion that she had encouraged Jake Ridley.

"Don't be absurd. But next time you want a bit of relaxation, don't fob me off with all that rubbish about getting dinner and then go seeking out some other male. Exactly what you said you'd never do, if I remember rightly. You might not care for me particularly, but you'll be safe with me. And you can come along any time you like."

With him—and Isobel. Rennie didn't answer. She went to find refuge in the kitchen—and dinner preparations.

CHAPTER FIVE

THAT NIGHT AFTER DINNER Dev retired to the office to do some paperwork, and Isobel excused herself, too.

"I have to send some copy back to my boss and I've been so fascinated taking it all in I haven't really settled down to any solid work yet."

Aunt Nina took the opportunity to go to bed early, and Rennie was left with the indefatigable Grace, who was poring once more over country magazines and books on stud farming. Rennie found a chair on the veranda and sat in the half dark, determinedly not thinking of her adventure of the afternoon. Instead, she reflected how strange it was that she should be here in the Outback, looking up at a night sky where the stars were too big to be believable and the heavens were so close. She heard the echoing call of a mopoke owl, and from away out on the plains, a spine-chilling howl of a dingo. "Where the dingoes and crows won't molest me—" That brought her back to Jake Ridley.

What *would* have happened if Dev hadn't come along when he did? *Jake would have let me go,* she decided. *He wasn't cruel or vicious. Hungry in some way? Hurt, disillusioned? Like me.* Yet all that part of her life—her shattered love life—seemed a long way off. It seemed to have receded into a distance so great that she could no longer see it with eyes that recognized. It was all as unreal as a mirage. Jean-Yves, Peter Morgan—both of them seemed strangely unimportant. Part of a past that had led her here. To what?

She heard someone come into the sitting room, and Dr. Grace's voice said, "Sit down for a minute, Dev, for Pete's sake. I came all the way from Adelaide to talk business with you and you haven't yet given me a minute of your time. I don't intend to be ignored, and I meant it when I said I wouldn't give my agreement to your appointing Tim Lang manager of Silver Springs."

"Then tell me why," said Dev reasonably, and Rennie could hear the scrape of a chair as he sat down. "Go on, talk away."

Grace did. She told Dev that she had made a thorough investigation of Silver Springs while she was there. "I drove over the property from one boundary to the other and I kept my eyes open. I also examined the books. And the thing that struck me most forcibly was that matters are not what they were in father's day. We used to carry twice as much stock in the old days. I could tell just by looking at it. So what's happened? Don't the stockmen muster the scrub anymore? Doesn't anyone keep the bore pumps working so that all the paddocks can be used? I saw at least three bores that were idle. Oh, I know it had all become too much for the old man in the last few years of his life, but why doesn't this young fellow get off his backside and get the place into full working order again? He must be both ignorant and incompetent, Dev. And even you must admit he's irresponsible, as well. What sort of a person would have let a girl like Rennald Baxter jump out of the Cessna over Nimmitibel as he did the other day?"

Rennie, who had been no more than half listening, heard that and felt herself writhe. Before she had thought twice, she was on her feet and at the doorway. Directly opposite her, she saw Dev leaning back in an armchair.

His lips twisted wryly as he said, "I blame myself more than Tim for that. And I'm not at all sure, given the same set of circumstances, that I wouldn't have done exactly as he did. Charm can be a very powerful persuader. She has quite a way with her, that cook of yours." He smiled straight across at Rennie, his eyes glinting oddly, and she felt her cheeks flame.

Dr. Grace turned with a frown and saw her there, and Rennie said flatly, "Excuse me for interrupting, but I thought I should let you know that I'm sitting just outside the door."

"For goodness' sake, we know that," said Grace impatiently. "Do be quiet. I'm trying to talk to Dev and God knows, everyone seems intent on making it impossible. Don't you start, too, Rennald."

"Stop hanging in space, Rennald," said Dev. He fished in his pocket and tossed her a packet of cigarettes and a box of matches, both of which she managed to catch. "Light yourself a cigarette and sit down where we can all see you. We'll watch our tongues if we should need to." There was mockery in his glance and a note in his voice that dared her to disobey.

She sat down and made a business of lighting a cigarette. Dev proceeded laconically and lightly to deal with his aunt.

"Now as to how the station's run, Grace—what the hell do you think you know about it? These investigations of yours . . . you wouldn't know the first thing to start looking for, so don't try to fool me. You might learn a thing or two reading my books, but it won't be worth anything to you because they're not specifically concerned with this particular part of the Outback. And you know damn all about the Silver Springs district."

"I was born at Silver Springs," retorted Grace. "I

spent my girlhood there long before you were born, Nicholas.''

Nicholas? Rennie's eyes looked up quizzically. But of course that was Dev's name. Nicholas Deveraux.

''And how you hated it,'' he reminded her pleasantly. ''You couldn't wait to get away. I don't remember that you were ever a visitor during my boyhood. . . . In any case, the fact remains you know nothing about it. If you did, you'd realize that the ranch was drastically over-stocked in the early days. The old man learned sense later—when he found he was halfway to creating a desert in his back paddocks. God knows how many square miles of saltbush and mulga were all but destroyed because he persisted in overstocking. Too many bores, all the paddocks overgrazed, nothing left to fall back on when there was a drought.''

''The money came in,'' Grace argued. ''We never lacked for anything. The homestead's always been kept in good repair, nothing stinted. It was drought that killed the feed in those paddocks—drought and wind erosion. . . . It may not concern you greatly, Dev, because you have Nimmitibel to help fill your pockets, but now that I've retired from medicine I'm going to need all that my share in Silver Springs brings in and, as well, I have Nancy's future to think of. I want you to take over. You know the business.''

Dev uttered a long low laugh. It was not in the least related to Jake Ridley's way of laughing. It had a sort of melody, a throatiness in it, that fell softly on Rennie's ears, so that she smiled, too.

''Grace,'' he said. ''Since you've retired you don't know what to do with yourself, do you? Why don't you take another trip? What you get from Silver Springs is not going to make all that much difference in your life— you're hardly on the bread line, that's for sure. But don't get the idea you can come here running my life and preaching to me how things were done at Silver Springs when you were a girl. Times have changed. We've learned better how to treat the land since then. If I took over—which I have no intention of doing—I assure you you'd be no better pleased. So suppose you pipe down and leave it to me. Unless you prefer to buy out my share and take full responsibility?''

"Don't be so absolutely ridiculous," said Grace. She crossed her legs and looked at him in a hostile way. "The whole point is—Silver Springs is the family home. It's unthinkable to leave outsiders in possession—people to whom it means nothing, who don't care. Have you so entirely cut yourself off from decent living that family ties mean nothing to you?''

He blew out a cloud of cigarette smoke and his eyes narrowed. "Meg will look after the homestead just as she always has. As for me—Nimmitibel is my home. My maternal grandfather owned the property even if he didn't run it himself. I've been here a long while now, Grace, and I like it. I more than like it. In fact, I'd leave it only on one condition." He looked at the glowing tip of his cigarette, then leaned forward and ashed it carefully in a small copper ashtray, only that day cleaned to shining beauty by Rennie. "And that," he said, "would be if the girl I marry asks me to." He looked at her and he looked at Rennie, and his look said that the matter was closed. Then he added, "Talking of family, Grace, didn't I hear you say you were going to phone to see how Nancy's making out? In the enemy camp," he added with a little smile.

Grace said nothing, but she rose and left the room. Rennie got up from her chair, too.

"And where are *you* running off to?" he asked. By getting lazily to his feet, he managed to cut off her path very effectively, and she felt her heart begin a sudden wild pounding. She looked at him distrustfully, and he took a couple of steps closer to her. "Those daredevil eyes of yours are frightened," he remarked coolly. "What is there about being left alone with me to scare you? Surely it can't be the result of that little lecture I read you earlier on—"

She shook her head, looked at the cigarette half smoked in her fingers, and then as if under compulsion back at the face that was now not far from her own.

"Then for God's sake, can't we kiss and be friends?" His mouth was smiling but his eyes, dark in the subdued lamplight, seemed to Rennie to be deadly earnest. The phrase he had used made her flinch slightly. She didn't seem able to guard her reactions anymore. She had caught herself out more than once reading meanings into his words, his actions, that were simply not there. The fact was, she simply had no idea how to take him. She didn't know yet why he had invited her to Nimmitibel that first time they met; why, now, he had more or less threatened Grace and maneuvered her into staying after she had been tricked into coming; whether he simply needed a cook, or whether there was something more personal in it all, some sort of a challenge—a calling of what he thought might be her bluff about men, about the Outback.

Now he was watching her so intently that she felt completely confused. She knew that he was going to marry—his words of only a few minutes ago had told her that quite clearly. "I'll leave Nimmitibel on only one condition—if the girl I'm going to marry asks me to."

And now, "Kiss and be friends." Rennie was not going to jump to conclusions this time, to get upset about a casually worded offer of truce. She raised her eyebrows slightly and gave him a cool—a very cool—smile.

"If that's the way you want it, Mr. Deveraux."

He stood looking down at her in silence, his eyes quizzical. Rennie raised a hand that trembled slightly and put the cigarette to her lips. Then, unexpectedly, his fingers were around her wrist, her hand was snatched from her face, the cigarette flew out in an arc and she was being held in an inescapable grip, helpless against his body. Her lips burned under the brief force of his kiss, and when he relaxed his hold on her she pulled away and went to retrieve her cigarette from the carpet that was beginning to smolder. With the toe of her sandal, she rubbed at the black mark and gradually felt her breathing grow more normal.

"You might have set fire to the house," she said reproachfully.

"But not to you."

She shook her head. "Not to me." She almost added, "I've had enough of burning myself on sacrificial fires," but that sounded, even to her mental ear, overdramatic. And while she *had* had enough of it, if she wasn't pretty careful it just could happen again. She said, "It would be nice to think we were friends. But as your cook I'd rather hold you in respect—and dispense with the kissing."

She saw his jaw tighten and suddenly she could not bear to look at him a moment longer. She felt his lips, his body, against her own, and the fever of her other loves— unremembered when Jake had held her pinioned against the tree—had come back into her veins like sicktide. She didn't know what was happening to her and almost wished she could wake to another day and find this had been no more than a disturbing dream.

This time, when she attempted to pass him, he simply let her go.

THE NEXT MORNING Rennie heard Dr. Grace working on Isobel. She knew Dev's views now—his Achilles' heel—and she would make the most of her knowledge, and prime Isobel as to what she should demand before she would agree to marry Dev.

"You're being very Spartan, putting in a holiday here—even if it is a kind of working holiday. There's no real need for Dev to live here, you know; it's nothing but a self-imposed banishment. When he marries, he must—and of course he *will*—go back to Silver Springs where it's so much more comfortable. There's no danger of being cut off there when it rains, and there's blessed relief for the eyes from all this glaring red earth."

Isobel listened and smiled faintly, and then she said, "Oh, but I can quite understand why Dev loves it here, Dr. Warren. It's a fascinating place—it puts you under a spell so that you feel you could stay here forever." Rennie, setting the table for lunch, couldn't believe her ears. It hardly looked as though Grace were going to find an ally in Isobel. She should have been delighted, yet, instead, she had a curious feeling of deflation. "As a matter of fact," Isobel continued, "I've been promised a look at the muster and a couple of nights sleeping under the stars. I'm really thrilled at the prospect."

"I would calm down if I were you," advised Grace, dampening Isobel's enthusiasm. "I warn you, you'll be thoroughly fed up by the end of the day. You'll be sick of the dust and the heat and the flies—and the monotony."

Rennie went out to the kitchen. She felt horribly envious of Isobel. What would she not give to go out to muster and to sleep out under the stars? But she wouldn't have the chance. She wondered if Isobel would be looking for material for these articles she was supposed to be wrting, or if that was just a fiction, a cover-up in case she didn't after all want to marry Dev and live in the

Outback. Somehow she couldn't imagine Isobel turning Dev down.

Coming here, she decided, had been a mistake. Her life seemed to have no cohesion, she felt restless, dissatisfied, and if she had any sense she would get out. It was no use trying to fool herself: she was not going to influence the course of events out here, and it was not really her business whether Tim Lang got his managership or not. It was a matter that concerned Dev and Dr. Grace—and of course Isobel. She certainly couldn't force Dr. Grace to sign anything she didn't want to sign, nor could she persuade Isobel Sandison to do anything against her will.

That afternoon, while Isobel was changing into something suitable to accompany Dev out to check up on some bore pumps, Rennie went out to the citrus grove to pick some fruit for the dessert she was making for dinner. Dev came after her.

"I'm taking Isobel out to the muster camp tomorrow for a night or two. You'd better come along, Rennald Baxter."

"I can't," said Rennie matter-of-factly, as if she did not care in the least.

"Why not? I thought you were breaking your neck to see the Outback."

"I've got a job to do here." She reached up into a tree. There weren't many oranges left now, and she caught her hand on a thorn as she reached through the branches. She pulled the fruit, sucked at the thin line of red on the side of her hand, and looked at Dev with slight hostility.

He looked back at her and sunlight glinted on the thickness of his eyelashes and tipped them with gold.

"Cooking for Grace and Miss Sandison? To hell with that! If they can't stomach old Etta's efforts, what's to stop them from going into the house kitchen and mixing up an omelette or grilling a couple of steaks? I could manage that myself without difficulty.''

Rennie flushed. ''But I can't let Dr. Grace—''

''Of course you can. My aunt can't fairly claim she's engaged your service at Nimmitibel when for some strange ends of her own she made such an uproar about your coming here at all. I don't know whether or not she's paying you—I doubt whether you know either—and I certainly have never had any intentions of offering you monetary rewards. No matter what culinary or extra-culinary tasks you've felt obliged to shoulder.'' His blue eyes mocked her and she thought, *So he has noticed the cleaning and the polishing and the flowers.*

''To me,'' he said, and he screwed up his eyes and looked more mocking than ever, ''you are a guest—if a somewhat bizarre one. Nothing less.''

''Nothing less—and nothing more,'' she said unwisely.

''What more do you want to be?'' he asked with a dangerous smile.

She flushed deeply. ''Nothing at all.'' She turned her back on him and began to march toward the house. ''It's too hot to indulge in verbal battles with you, Mr. Deveraux.''

''Fine. We'll consider the matter settled. You'll come,'' he said peremptorily from behind her. 'I don't like taking along one woman on her own. And if you refused, then it would have to be Miss Sandison.''

So, thought Rennie ironically, that was why she was being asked along. Not for her own edification, as he had suggested. And of course she would go. Dev would have his own way. And she would be a fool to miss out on the experience, even if—even if she really preferred not to see too much of Mr. Nicholas Deveraux.

It was undeniably exciting to drive out to the muster the next day. Dev looked casual, tough, slant-hatted—

exactly like one of his own stockmen, with the sleeves of
his dark shirt rolled up, his legs encased in tight trousers
and stockman's boots. And Isobel was very smart and
efficient-looking, but feminine as well, in riding breeches
and an immaculate pink shirt, as pale and delicate as her
sleek blond hair. Her square-crowned hat was set perfectly straight on her head, its chin strap emphasizing the
pretty firmness of her chin. Out at the muster, she sat her
horse beautifully, and Rennie caught herself thinking,
"Wouldn't she!" She was the type who would do anything well if she set her mind to it. She had that cool,
capable look about her.

Rennie, who had no style at all on horseback, was
suddenly self-conscious of this fact. In her blue jeans and
tan shirt, she reflected that she looked more as if she
should be helping Jimmy with the cooking than riding
with Miss Isobel Sandison. When Dev, who had selected
the horses for the two girls, said, "You'd better come
along with us—I'll keep an eye on you," Rennie jacked
up. She had seen the expression on Isobel's face.

"I'd rather not, thank you," she said positively. "I'm
too much of an amateur—I'd only be a nuisance. I'm not
all that keen on riding around, anyhow."

Dev eyed her doubtfully, and she assumed her most
determined—or stubborn—expression. "Very well. But
Isobel has to get her copy, or her boss will think she's
loafing."

Isobel gave him a quick look from under the straight
brim of her hat. "Oh, Vince eats out of my hand. I can
take all the time I need," she said casually.

Rennie watched them ride off together, Isobel with her
straight back, her riding-school bearing; Dev casual,
comfortable, as though he lived most of his life on
horseback, which he probably did. She reflected briefly
on that last little exchange, wondered if Dev and Isobel

had learned something about each other from it. Did Dev want to find out if Isobel meant to go back? And was Isobel in answer implying that she needed a little longer to make up her mind?

Or was Rennie imagining all this?

She looked at the horse that Dev had picked out for her. Safe as a rocking horse, he had said. But she didn't believe that. That chestnut wouldn't be out here if he was rocking-horse standard. And if he got it into his head to join in the stockwork, would she be able to control him, to dissuade him? Isobel would. *I'll give it a try,* she decided suddenly. After all, it was not like Rennald Baxter to stand back timidly and refuse to try her hand at anything at all. And she could manage a horse within limits. It was just a matter of experience—and of forgetting that you didn't have any style. Mainly it had been the thought of tagging along with those other two, an unwanted third, that had held her back.

So another few minutes found her cantering through the trees toward the cloud of dust out on the flats.

Soon she forgot her self-consciousness. Her hat was hanging down her back and the chestnut was a little beauty, lively but obedient—just her kind of mount, in fact. She rode around keeping her distance from the great growing mob of cattle that the musters were bringing in. Dev and Isobel had taken their horses into the shade of some trees at the base of a long scrub-covered ridge. Rennie kept well away from them, but she could see that Dev was pointing out something to Isobel, who was watching with interest as the stockmen came riding in with little herds of beasts—sometimes no more than three, sometimes as many as ten or twelve. The herd on the flat was being held by a few station hands who rode around the outside, slowly and watchfully.

Rennie had reined in her horse and was ambling

slowly along while she watched and tried to work out for herself what it was all about. She gave a small start of surprise when Jake Ridley's voice said from behind her. "Hello, Rennie! You okay? The boss said you aren't a keen horsewoman."

He came cantering up and then slowed down to keep pace with her. Rennie looked across at him cautiously. She hadn't seen him since that day by the water and she wasn't sure how to greet him. But here in the middle of the muster, she was quite safe. His cold green eyes were looking at her unblinkingly, and she decided that the best thing to do was to act as if it had never happened.

She said lightly, "I'm managing. I'd be a fool if I didn't with a horse like this."

"Yes. Pokataroo's a good little horse. Why don't you forget your inhibitions and come along with me? I'll look after you and show you a bit of action."

Rennie considered for a moment. Maybe Dev wouldn't approve, but good heavens, what was she thinking of? Where on earth was the harm in riding around with the head stockman? She nodded, and he said instantly, but awkwardly, like a man who is not used to apologizing, "I'm sorry for what happened the other day. I shouldn't have manhandled you. It won't happen again."

"Forget it," she said, and sent him a forgiving smile.

She had a great time after that, following him into the scrub while he hunted up some beasts resting in the shade, obeying his shouted instructions—"Stay where you are!" or "Get around behind me," or "Come in from the side there and head him off!" She knew it was only make-believe, that she wasn't really being a help, but it was exhilarating and she was sure that if she were taken seriously at a muster—if she were properly instructed—she would soon learn to be of use. She watched with admiration the way Jake—and most of the stock-men—would wheel their horses around so tightly that they leaned almost to the ground, and her heart thrilled to the wild excitement of it all.

She was dusty and sweating and she had almost forgotten Isobel and Dev when Jake came galloping out of the scrub in pursuit of a great white bull that lumbered clumsily ahead, its huge head swinging from side to side. This time, she knew instinctively that she must keep right out of the way. That white bull looked so immense, so fearsome, she would not have been surprised to see smoke and flames coming out of its nostrils. She held her breath as Jake pursued it through the trees and drove it into the open. It was snorting and bellowing, and he was close on its tail as it charged across the flat, turning this way and that as if seeking a means of escape. Then suddenly he was beside it—a sight that made him gasp aloud—and he had left the saddle and was swinging on the great bull's tail. Another second, and the beast was down in the dust. Jake had its back legs secured in a strap, she saw the flash of a knife, there was a moment's work, then Jake was back on his horse and the bull was struggling to its feet, bellowing with rage and pain.

Rennie rode out from the fringe of trees. There was a general movement toward the camp for lunch, Isobel was on her own and Dev had ridden over to join Jake. She saw the two men disappear together into the trees that screened the camp. She wondered if Dev was pleased with Jake . She had a strong feeling that the bull had been no ordinary beast.

She caught up with Isobel and asked her, "Did Dev tell you what that was all about?"

Isobel, she couldn't help noticing, looked quite ex-hausted, and though her face was flushed with the heat, it was certainly not streaked with dust as Rennie knew her own face must be. Her hat was still firmly on her head and her blond hair was neat, but it required an obvious effort for her to continue to keep her back straight. Rennie had lost the ribbon from her hair and she knew she must look a sight. She grabbed the hat that was hanging down her back and crammed it onto her head, because the sun was high in the sky and its heat was striking down like fire.

Isobel told her briefly, disparagingly, "Some old scrub bull."

"Jake—castrated it, didn't he?"

Isobel bit her lip in distaste. "I presume so. Dev didn't say. He was furious."

"Furious?" Rennie felt amazed. "But why? Surely he wouldn't want a wild bull like that as a breeder—"

The other girl shrugged. "There were other things the head stockman should have been seeing to. That show was obviously put on for your benefit. It wouldn't have happened if you hadn't been such an obviously admiring audience."

Rennie looked at her speechlessly.

"Your stockman," said Isobel, "has ways of courting that are as crude as he is himself." She suddenly touched her mount's flank with her heels and galloped off.

Lunch was beef and vegetables and billy tea by the gallon. And then it was back to work. Dev, who had not spoken to Rennie, came to tell the girls, "Jimmy's going to mix up a damper and cook it in a bedourie oven. That's something you must see, Isobel. You can come back over to the muster when you've watched him, right?"

"Marvelous," said Isobel, but her smile was strained.

Rennie asked, "What's a bedourie oven?"

"If you stick around you'll find out," said Dev. His eyes looked hard and more than a little angry, and

Rennie expected to hear, "Keep away from my head stockman." It came, sure enough. "You might keep it in mind, Rennald, if you don't want to come around with me, not to incite my head stockman to any further demonstrations of valor. I don't relish the thought of broken bones—or worse."

Rennie flushed angrily. "I had nothing to do with what Jake did! I didn't ask him to swing on any bull's tail. But," she added, "I thought he was magnificent. Besides, you don't want to keep that old beast as a breeder, surely."

His look sharpened. "Did you think that up for yourself?"

"It's common sense, isn't it?"

He shrugged his broad shoulders. "Maybe. But Jake knows my orders about scrubbers—that one in particular." And then he was gone.

Deliberately, Rennie put him out of her mind. She strolled over to watch Jimmy mixing up the flour and soda and water for the damper in an outsize basin. Then he scraped the mixture into a huge aluminum pot, put the lid on it, set it in a hole that was filled with hot ashes and piled more ashes and earth over the top of it.

"Will it be good?" she asked him.

He grinned and closed one eye. "You bet! She'll be beaut—if she's eaten fresh. You'll see at tucker time."

Rennie looked around to see what Isobel thought. She had been so interested watching Jimmy that she had forgotten about Isobel. And Isobel simply wasn't there. The heat and the dust and the effort of keeping up appearances had, it seemed, completely defeated her.

Rennie found her back in the small tent that had been erected for the girls, sitting on her bedding roll, her face in her hands.

"Aren't you coming back to the muster?" she asked.

"If I do," said Isobel, "I'll become totally manic. Besides, there's nothing new to see. It will be the same performance as this morning."

"I don't think so," said Rennie after a moment. "That mob they've mustered—it must be for a reason."

"To pick out the fats," said Isobel tiredly. "The beasts to send to the saleyards."

"Don't you want to watch?"

"I can imagine it. . . . Why don't you forget it too, and we can take a swim in the pool."

"We can do that later," said Rennie. "I'm going to watch them cutting out the fats."

Isobel's light blue eyes watched her calculatingly and a little cattily. "*Who* is it you want to watch? That brutish stockman with his horrible knife? Or—"

Rennie knew she had colored, but she looked back at Isobel unblinkingly. "Don't worry, I'm not trying to steal Dev from you."

The other girl's lip curled. "Do you think you could?"

"I'm quite sure I couldn't." Rennie turned away abruptly. She splashed her face with cold water at the plastic basin that stood on a box and was to serve for their ablutions. When she had toweled her face dry she applied a liberal coat of protective cream to it. It was certainly hot—hotter than the morning had been, the atmosphere oppressive, tense, as if it were building up to something. A storm, she wondered. To see rain—to feel it—would be fantastic. She brushed out her hair, grimacing a little at its stiffness, for it was thick with dust, then tied it back firmly from her neck with a yellow ribbon. When she turned around again, Isobel had stripped herself down to panties and bra, kicked open her bedding roll and flung herself down on the thin mattress. Her eyes were closed, her arms held away from her sides for coolness. She looked singularly out of place, with her long pale limbs, in these particular surroundings. *As I must too,* mused Rennie. But her limbs were covered against the heat and dust by her long-sleeved tan shirt and the legs of her blue jeans. She looked down at Isobel for a moment and then said dryly, "I'll tell Dev you're working on your notes, shall I?"

Isobel's eyes flew open. "Don't go out of your way to tell him anything."

Rennie got the idea. Isobel was not to be used as an excuse for seeking Dev out. She put on her hat and went outside to find the chestnut horse again. She couldn't wait to be back at the muster.

This time, Jake left her alone. Everyone left her alone, as a matter of fact, except Dev, who came to ask, "Where's Isobel? Wallowing in the water hole? Or has she gone to ground?"

"She's writing up her notes."

He looked at her for a moment, his gaze traveling slowly over her slim figure, her face that was perspiring slightly under the shade of the wide-brimmed hat. She met his eyes for a disconcerting second, looked over his shoulder and spotted Jake. The change in her expression made him look around.

"You're not going to chase around with my head stockman this afternoon, Rennald Baxter. He's got work to do. Understand? And I've warned him not to waste his time and mine taking unnecessary risks to entertain and encourage an already foolhardy girl."

"A bloody-minded wildcat of a girl," enlarged Rennie, eyes flashing, annoyed with his treatment of her. Jake, after all, must know what he was doing. He had decidedly not thrown that bull to amuse her.

But Dev had something more to say to her and he stayed to say it, ignoring her retort.

"I don't pretend to know anything about the state of

your heart, Miss Baxter—or even if you are in possession of one—but Jay Ridley is a man with very sharp edges, as you will no doubt discover if you continue to amuse yourself with him. You may like courting danger, but this is an insidious danger—and you just might cut yourself right through to the heart.''

He gave her a long steady unnerving look from his very blue eyes. Somehow she felt there was more danger to her from those eyes than from anything she had ever experienced in the whole of her life. . . . And then he had got back into the saddle, wheeled the black horse and galloped over to the muster once more.

Rennie sought the trees, dismounted and stood in the shade. Her back against a tree trunk, she kept her eyes closed for a long time. When she opened them again she could see before her the great red sandy plain spread out flatly. Away on the horizon was a line of flat-topped ridges, purple against the sky, yet not as clear-cut as they had been in the morning. No, they were blurred to dullness, and she wondered if it was dust or rain that blew around them. The cattle were restless, bellows rent the air, stockwhips cracked, the dust rose forming a thick enveloping cloud.

She had no idea how long she stood motionless, watching. No one took any notice of her, and though she had more or less expected that Jake Ridley would sooner or later find his way back to her, he didn't. Not that it mattered. She hadn't come out here to be noticed by anyone—just to watch. And watching had become automatic, compulsive, mindless, except that she was aware of urgency. The fats were being cut out of the mob and driven over to form a smaller mob, and it all seemed to be happening faster than she had expected. It was almost as if she were watching a movie that had been speeded up slightly. One stockman became the same as another, faceless, unidentifiable in the swirling red dust as some recalcitrant beast was wheeled away from the herd he was bellowing to rejoin. Sometimes she thought she was watching Dev, sometimes it seemed to be Jake, but it could have been anyone at all. Dust flew and thickened, the heat grew oppressive and Rennie, flat against her tree trunk, felt she had fallen under some kind of a spell and would never move again.

The rough bark of the tree was bruising her spine through the cotton shirt; somehow the yellow ribbon she had tied so firmly had slipped off her hair which now hung suffocatingly against her perspiring neck. Yet she simply could not make the effort to move. She stood and leaned and watched in a mindless daze, and slowly the whole world seemed to become a heavy dull pink color, its central point the cloud around the stock with its merry-go-round of flying horsemen.

And then—with a literally electrifying suddenness—the sky was split open by a tremendous sheet of lightning. The tree against which she leaned shuddered in the furious roll of thunder that followed, and Rennie was fairly jerked upright to witness a stampede rush as pandemonium broke loose in the herd. The terrified beasts milled about frantically, bellowing in fright and panic, and then they were all charging in one direction, hooves thudding, the dust flying so thickly as to almost obliterate them from sight.

A horseman streaked past as Rennie stood wide-eyed, then another and another. Stockwhips cracked and every living thing on the plain raced in the one direction—all except the girl under the trees. Rennie didn't know if it was thunder she heard or the pounding of hooves.

She saw the black horse go past, a flying streak, with Dev crouching over his neck. Her heart was in her mouth as she watched him race like some demon—or some god—to the front of the panic-stricken herd as it thudded along like one monstrous whole. Long stockwhip snaking, cracking, he rode right into the path of the maddened beasts. She closed her eyes, sure that he must be trampled to death. . . .

When she dared to look again, the leaders had turned, Dev's stockwhip cracked out like a pistol, they swung around, and in a moment the rush was broken, the herd was ringing, the merry-go-round of stockmen was on the move again.

It was an amazing sight to witness. Gradually the dust and confusion subsided, and the cattle slowed down, their sides heaving, eyes still rolling, heads and horns tossing still in fright.

She was standing staring, fascinated, her heart pounding, when Dev appeared out of the dust, his hat tipped back on his head, his nostrils flaring. His blue eyes looked down at her in astonishment from a face that was a mask of red dust.

"So you're still with us, Rennald Baxter!"

"Why not?" said Rennie jauntily. It was like heaven to see him still alive, to hear his voice. She knew all her color had gone—she had been terrified for him—but she was certain he didn't know, because there must be a coat of dust as thick and concealing on her face as there was on his. She managed an impudent smile. "Do you imagine I'd walk out on a show like that? I thought you were going to be trampled to death riding out there the way you did, Mr. Deveraux. I crossed my fingers for you, I really did! You put up a magnificent performance!" She added with an innocent widening of her eyes, "I do hope it wasn't solely for my benefit."

He stared, his mouth twisted wryly and for an instant there was a spark of laughter deep in his eyes. Then he told her sardonically, "I'm sorry to disappoint you—

somehow it slipped my mind you were standing there alone and unprotected. Well, I'm glad you've survived. And enjoyed the spectacle. Good day!'' He touched the brim of his hat mockingly with the tip of his stockwhip handle, wheeled around and was gone.

CHAPTER SIX

AFTER THAT, Rennie didn't want to stay. She felt just a little bit sick. She knew that the afternoon's work had come unstuck, that all those beasts so meticulously cut out from the herd were now back where they started.

She found Pokataroo and rode back to the camp. A few big drops of rain had fallen and evaporated instantly. A wind had come sweeping through the trees, and down at the little water hole beyond the camp Isobel was—as Dev had put it—wallowing in the water. Rennie got into her swimsuit and joined her. They stayed there till sunset. The sky had cleared somewhat. There were clouds far out on the horizon and a haze of dust in the air, but no more rain. The heat persisted in full force.

Rennie lingered behind Isobel as they went back in silence to the tent to dress. This dull dusty sunset light was something new. The indigo shadows on the ground had a smokiness about them, and the air had become intensely still. Soon the cockatoos and parrots came screeching and screaming down over the trees to the water, and the soft old rose light sharpened briefly to glowing vermilion, so that suddenly every tree, every leaf, every spike of grass and stone stood out sharp and fiery and vibrantly clear. And then, as though a great light had been switched off, it was all over.

Oh, God, how heartbreakingly beautiful it all was, thought Rennie.

With the darkness, the air cooled down. The stockmen came back to the camp weary and dusty, cleaned up and came to the camp fire for dinner with shining faces. Isobel was her calm smiling self once more, and Rennie felt so weary that she could have fallen asleep at the drop of a hat.

The damper   an enormous flattish loaf—was produced and admired, and Rennie ate a great buttered slab of it with her dish of stew, ladled out from the gigantic pot that Jimmy had cooked up over the fire. There was billy tea, and all the men had a prodigious thirst. Stars hung bright in the blackness of the sky, and apart from the crackling of the fire, the lazy talk and laughter of the men and the occasional distant bellowing of the cattle, the night was still and peaceful. Dev had come to sit on the ground near Isobel and Rennie, to smoke and to ask Isobel how she had put in the afternoon. His eyes glittered in the firelight, and in its reflected glow, his face looked warmly tan. For some reason, Rennie could not keep her eyes off him. He was not glamorously handsome like Jake, but his face was stronger and had far more character, she thought hazily.

Isobel made much of the fact that she had a heap of material to deal with, to arrange. She had been quite carried away writing up her notes, and then that weird rainless storm had come, and she had missed the cutting out completely. She kept her eyes on Dev's face as she talked, and Rennie looked away from the desire that was there so plain to see—the invitation in the curve of her lips, the softness of her voice, the way she leaned her slender body toward him. She might not wholeheartedly enjoy a day's mustering, but she was certainly madly in love with Dev Deveraux.

Rennie got up abruptly and wandered away. She couldn't sit there any longer and see those eyes of

Isobel's, usually so cool, devouring Dev, telling him that
here she was and that she wanted him.

He would leave all of this for her. He would leave
Nimmitibel even though he loved it and it was so
beautiful. Rennie hated the thought of his going.
"Because of Tim," she reminded herself, "and Meg." It
wouldn't be fair to them.

She went down toward the water hole where the
shapes of trees stood darkly, twisted and ancient, silent
guardians of the Outback. She wasn't disturbed or startled when Jake appeared, and if Dev had noticed him
coming after her, then she didn't care. But Dev had been
so wrapped up in Isobel Sandison that he had scarcely
noticed Rennie going. She needed someone to talk to,
and Jake had promised her that he wouldn't "manhan-
dle" her again.

Everything was fine for a while. They talked about the
muster, the stampede, the electric storm, and he told her
that they had gone through the whole business of cutting
out fats again. Then she asked him about the stars in the
southern sky, and they moved into the open so he could
point out the Southern Cross. And suddenly, disconcert-
ingly, the conversation was personal, and it was Jake
who had made it so.

"It's weird standing here in the dark with you—and
liking it. I thought I'd given women up for good—women
like you, decent women. But you've got right under my
skin. You're different. You don't look at me with those
greedy knowing eyes—summing me up as a marriage bet,
maybe passing me over that way but still thinking I
might be good for a game of temptation. I often remember how you got on with folding up your parachute that
day we first met. I stood and watched you, and even
beyond your courage and your daring, I thought you
were great. And that's not like me! Then I went too far

when I met you next. God knows why. I cursed myself for it afterward. Dispensing with the preliminaries and thinking I could do what I liked with your sort of girl. . . .You don't still hold it against me, do you?"

"No," she said awkwardly, wishing that he would not talk to her like this. "But I was sorry it happened."

"Well, I've apologized, haven't I? And behaved myself perfectly tonight."

"Yes." She sent him a troubled smile, glimpsed that fantastically handsome face in the blueness of the starlight, the feathery shadows of trees flickering over his back and shoulders and the darkness of his hair, and she shivered a little. His eyes, black smudges in the night, were on her face, unfathomable, strangely animal in that they seemed to send her no message, no communication, no feeling of warmth.

A little silence fell between them. Through a thin line of trees, she could see the flickering glow of the camp fire and hear one of the stockman playing the mouth organ. He had chosen the tune that she had heard Jake whistling, melancholy yet gravely gay, a disturbing background now to Jake's voice as he said, "I could do with a girl like you, you know that? Someone to drag me out of this . . . spiritual hell I've somehow created for myself on God's earth."

She felt a coldness, a tremor of apprehension at his words. His eyes told her nothing, but his lips were telling her too much.

"You're a girl I could believe in, a loyal sort of a girl who wouldn't stab me in the back, who—" his voice was suddenly full of violence "—who hasn't the remotest conception of what cheating and trickery and double-dealing in love are all about." He paused and it was on the tip of her tongue to argue that he was quite wrong, that she knew all about double-dealing in love, when his next words threw her right off balance. "Have you ever loved a man, Renniebird?"

The name, the endearment, shocked her first, and then the quick color stained her cheeks and ebbed away as she realized what he meant by his question. He wasn't asking if she had ever been in love: he was asking something quite different. And suddenly she was aware that her own experiences in love had been very limited, very innocent. This tough worldly stockman would laugh at her if she were to pour out to him the tale of her betrayal by Jean-Yves, by Pete Morgan, both of whom she had thought she loved and who had been playing lighthearted games with her. She suspected that any games Jake Ridley engaged in would be far from lighthearted.

She shook her head, not looking at him. They had begun to move slowly back into the shadows of the trees, without her even being aware of it. He put his arm lightly around her waist, and she felt herself tense. She could hear Dev Deveraux asking her, "What kind of—God knows, *innocent*—love affair has given you your suspicious outlook on men?" To drown out the memory, she said, "I haven't had a lot to do with love."

"Then come and have a lesson." His voice was low and indistinct and before she knew it she was in his arms and his mouth was demandingly on hers.

She fought herself free of him furiously, her breath coming fast, and when he let her go suddenly, she heard him swearing softly and hideously at himself and she mentally blocked her ears.

"I'm going back to the camp," she breathed, but as she turned his hand shot out to hold her back.

"I'm sorry. I'll leave you alone. I swear it. I'm just out of practice when it comes to conducting a civilized relationship with a woman. Can't we talk a little longer so I can prove to you—and to myself—that I'm not completely . . . Neanderthal?''

She managed a shaky smile, but her heart was hammering and his grip was like a steel trap. She said with an attempt at calm, "If you—if you pounce on me again, I'll yell at the top of my voice. You talk about needing a woman you can trust. What about me? As it happens, I'm not looking for any sort of a man right now, but if I were, it would certainly not be someone like you, who—"

"Give me another chance," he said with a bitter intensity. He let go of her and she didn't move. Running away from danger had never been her line. She watched him find cigarettes, light one with a hand that was obviously shaking, put out the match meticulously. He took a long draw, exhaled smoke and looked at her warily in the starlit darkness.

"You're not going to take your chance and run away from me? Well, that's a break. I guess I'm not a likable man—and I blame a woman for that—the woman it was my bad luck to marry. A goodly apple rotten at the core, filthy rotten. She played the field, made a complete fool of me and finally left me. That, in a nutshell, is the story of my disillusionment, of how I was kicked out of an Eden that proved to have been the equivalent of the old chestnut, a fool's paradise. And that, Rennie, is why I gave away the civilization bit and came here to sweat out a life I no longer valued in the Outback."

"I'm sorry," said Rennie after a moment. It occurred to her that he had left out a very vital part of his story, but she could guess at it. He must have idolized the woman who had ruined his life.

He drew on his cigarette. "She's still somewhere around, I guess. But not in this state. Probably living with some man or another. We're not divorced—that wouldn't matter to Norma. And me, I just never wanted to set eyes on another female in my life." She felt his eyes seek her face and could imagine their cold greenness. "Then you came along. And I seem to have been doing my best to teach you to hate me when it's the very opposite I want. Could be as well you're just a bird of passage out here—otherwise I might really set out to persuade you to forget that I already have a wife."

She shook her head. He would never be able to do that. Plenty of girls these days seemed willing to dispense with the marriage bond in their relationships with men, but she could never think that way. To her, the spiritual values added by vows made solemnly in a church were too important. And all that apart, she knew she would never fall in love with Jake. In a strange way, she liked him despite his very obvious defects and she was beginning to feel a kind of personal concern for him. If he felt he was in a spiritual hell, then he needed help and understanding, but she couldn't offer either if he were going to grab her every time they met.

She said, "I'm hard to persuade, Jake, so don't even try. And now I really am tired. I'd like to go back to the camp."

"I won't try to stop you. But will you promise that we can meet again and talk?"

"So long as you remember your promise."

"I'll remember. Tomorrow then?"

"Tomorrow," she agreed.

To her relief, he let her walk back alone. She gave the camp fire a wide berth, but she searched among the silhouettes of the men who sat around smoking, drinking mugs of tea, yarning.

Of Dev and Isobel there was not a sign.

She reached the tent, and Isobel was not there either. She made herself ready for bed and laid out her bedding roll under the trees nearby. It was marvelous to sleep out under a sky as vast and close and starry as this one. Physically, she felt as relaxed and comfortable as a cat in her bedding roll, but mentally she was restless and disturbed. She thought of Jake Ridley's wife who had destroyed his faith in women and wondered what his life had been before he exiled himself to the rough, hard existence of a stockman in the Outback. Did his wife have any inkling of the fact that she had twisted a man's whole mental outlook out of shape, as well as the course of his life? He must have loved her to excess to have become so embittered, so harsh. Her thoughts somehow switched to Dev Deveraux. Did he love Isobel like that, she wondered, and she couldn't answer her own question. Somehow, she couldn't imagine Dev putting himself so much at the mercy of another human being. His character was too strong.

It was of Dev she dreamed that night. In her dream they were floating in the hot sunny air together, under canopies that were like beautiful flowers, hers white, his the blue of his eyes, the blue of heaven. She reached out her hand to him, but before he could take it her canopy had collapsed and she was falling while his voice floated down to her, a strange disembodied megaphone voice, like the voice of a jump instructor, "I told you to keep a hold of me. I told you to forget Jake Ridley—''

She woke sweating to find that the sky was still high above her and she was safe on the ground in her bedding roll. She kept quite still until her heart had stopped its pounding and then she turned on her side and saw another figure sleeping on the ground not far away. Isobel, she thought, and fell asleep again.

She woke at dawn to see the light creeping into the vast sky, to listen to the silence, to watch a few shreds of gauzy cloud drift slowly, slowly over. And then, screeching and chattering, the birds came flying over—white corellas, rose-flushed galahs, small brightly colored finches. They came like leaves blown by an unseen wind and settled in the trees before they rose again. Now she could hear the cattle, the neighing of horses, the tinkle of condamine bells. And away over there, someone was stirring up the fire.

She knew it was Dev, though she wasn't sure why she was so certain. His back was toward her in the eerie colorless light, and he was painted in monochrome—the presiding spirit of the camp. He was there somehow or other when the horses were being caught and saddled, when the steaks were sizzling and the billy was on the boil; when the cook was mixing the damper; when the dust was in a red cloud above a herd of cattle, when the lightning split the heavens open; when the camp fire glowed red and the end of the day had come. Yes, he belonged out here as surely as the sun belonged in the sky, and it would be wrong, wrong, wrong for him to leave this for any woman, no matter how much he loved her. . . .

She stirred, sat up and scrambled quietly out of the blankets. While she was pulling on her boots and reflecting that this was the first time in her life that she had slept all night practically fully clad, she noticed that there was no bedding roll where she had seen one last night. Was Isobel up already, perhaps somewhere over there with Dev? Moving stealthily so as not to catch his eye, she made for the little tent.

Isobel was there, blond hair tangled, her bedding rumpled as though she had not slept well, a look of strain and even misery on her usually calm face. Quietly, Rennie stripped off her tan shirt, poured water from the plastic flask into the basin and washed. She got into the spare shirt she had brought—a blue one—brushed out her hair and tied it back.

When she emerged again the sun had come up over the horizon and the whole world was washed in a brilliant orange red light. Rennie stood perfectly still. It was like ... like pushing a door and discovering it opened onto paradise—an unimaginable visual and emotional delight. Her eyes, which had so often been charmed by the cool and pleasant greens of the English countryside, had discovered a new and intoxicating pleasure—the red sun of morning burnishing a land of red sand where trees stretched out long motionless cobalt shadows and the leaves hung still and glistening and translucently red bronze. It was a curiously crystalline moment—its perfection made absolute by the figure of the man moving through his own beautiful world toward her, while behind him, and beyond the stockman's camp now stirring to life, she could see his shining horse etched in black.

In that moment—fleetingly—she knew exactly how she felt about Dev Deveraux. And she was both exhilarated and appalled.

The brilliance of the light had softened quickly to a color less dramatic when he greeted her.

"You're certainly up with the birds, Rennald. Want a cup of tea?"

"That would be wonderful," said Rennie. She added, realizing only later that the silly lie was a defense mechanism, "I thought you were Jake."

"Indeed?" His eyes hardened instantly and his voice was cold. "Well, I won't point out the obvious inference to be drawn from that little error. . . . However, I'm afraid you'll have to accept the unpalatable fact that you won't be seeing much of my head stockman today. I'm sending you back to the homestead as soon as you've breakfasted."

Her feeling of disappointment was so strong as to be

shocking. And she knew that it centered on Dev. Not to be able to listen to his voice, even though it might be reviling her, was unbearable.

"Why?" she asked furiously.

He tilted his eyebrows maddeningly. "Do you really think I have to account for my decisions to you? Let's just say that I find it a little too much to have two disturbing females in the camp. One disrupted day is enough."

Rennie, standing not three feet away from him, flung up her head. "I suppose you were doing a bit of . . . supervising last night, even when you were so wrapped up in Isobel. You must have eyes in the back of your head, Mr. Deveraux. You're a regular—a regular cyclops!"

"And you are more than a little confused, Rennald Baxter," he said smoothly, maddeningly. "I advise you to put in some time on your Greek mythology when you have the opportunity."

"And I advise *you* to make up your mind what you want next time, Mr. Deveraux, before you start throwing invitations around."

His blue gaze narrowed and he took a step toward her. "Exactly what do you mean by that?"

She blinked. It was going a little too far to call it an invitation when you were asked along because it was bad policy to bring one girl on her own out to the muster. . . . She shrugged and made no reply.

"Sure you're not making insinuations about Isobel?"

"Quite sure," she said, disconcerted.

"Then that's fine. Isobel is having a great time, I assure you." He turned and with an abrupt, "Come over to the camp when you want your cup of tea," he strode away from her.

Rennie stood where she was for a moment. A great time. Well, she was not sure that Isobel had been having a great time yesterday in the heat and dust, but she surely had been having a great time last night. And Rennie's heart was wrung with an ignoble and insupportable feeling of jealousy. . . .

Dev commissioned one of the men to drive the two girls back to Nimmitibel homestead after they had breakfasted. They didn't talk on the way. Rennie made one or two attempts to start a conversation that she knew at best would be only a polite one, but Isobel wasn't interested. She wondered what was going on in the other girl's head, and she had the distinct feeling that Isobel didn't mind at all that their visit to the muster had been cut short.

Of one thing she was quite sure, and that was that Isobel was crazy about Dev. Was she becoming a little panic-stricken at the thought of all that went with him? That red sand and wilderness, that vast emptiness, that silence, that disappearing for perhaps days at a time into a man's world . . . .

When the jeep had dropped them off and they were on their way across the yard toward the house, she ventured to express her own disappointment that their stay had been curtailed and was stunned by Isobel's reaction.

"Well, it's all your fault. What did you expect, playing up to that stockman the way you did?"

"And what about you?" flared Rennie, whose nerves were ragged for one reason or another. "Two disturbing females, Dev said."

"Did he?" Isobel sounded faintly amused. "Disturbing, in my case, could have a slightly different connotation, though I hesitate to point it out to you if you're too self-centered and bone-headed to see it for yourself. I'm not just here on a job, in case you hadn't realized it. Dev asked me to come to see how I would adjust."

"And how do you adjust?" Rennie asked, annoyed at the way her heart was behaving. They had reached the long strip of shade made by the windbreak of an old saltbush, and they walked slowly as if each of them had something to say or to find out.

"I'm fascinated," said Isobel. She seemed to bite the words out. "All the same, Grace Warren is right—a woman has to consider the possible dangers in being cut off when the rivers flood and the rains come."

"You'll . . . you'll ask him to go to Silver Springs, then—to turn Tim Lang and his mother out?" Despite herself, there was a note of accusation in Rennie's voice, and Isobel's fine eyebrows lifted.

"Tim Lang is the son of a former head stockman," she said coldly. "His mother was housekeeper and cook to Dev's grandfather. As I see it, Dev is at liberty to make whatever changes he likes in his staff, and even you must have heard Dr. Warren say that the place is badly run. Of course," she continued before Rennie had time to protest, "if Tim is so drastically attached to Silver Springs, there's no reason why he shouldn't stay on and work there, or come to that, why Mrs. Lang shouldn't continue with the cooking. But in my view, any man worth his salt would get out and make his own way in life instead of taking the easy way and cashing in on the sentiment of old ties."

Rennie stopped dead still and looked at Isobel. "I thought you were a friend of Tim's sister."

"Of Lynette's? So I am. She's on the art staff of the paper I work for and I respect her for her ability and for her integrity," stated Isobel calmly. "But she's not a hanger-on at Silver Springs. She's had the character to make her own way instead of hanging on to the coat tails of the Deveraux family."

No more was said, but Rennie climbed the veranda steps feeling more upset than she had any right to be. If Isobel had made up her mind she wanted to live on Silver

Springs, then nothing was going to stop her. Because for the girl he loved, Dev would leave Nimmitibel, and it was Isobel he had invited to his home. . . .

Rennie received quite a welcome at Nimmitibel, from both Dr. Grace and Nina Sandison. Life, it seemed, would become at least part way civilized now that Grace's cook was back and they could sit down to an enjoyable dinner. She made a special effort that night—it kept her mind occupied and came up with a menu that really earned some praise, though Dev was not there to enjoy it. Dr. Grace plainly and simply relished her food, and Aunt Nina, as it was an all-woman occasion, became quite voluble, insisting on knowing the name of each dish and questioning Rennie closely on exactly how it was made. Finally Isobel said on a bored note, "Really, Aunt Nina, anyone would think you intended going home to your little flat and spending your whole time in the kitchen. And you won't, you know. You'll continue to eat out at your favorite cafés and restaurants as you've always done."

Nina looked slightly crestfallen and Rennie said cheerfully, "Never mind, Miss Sandison. Even if you never make the chocolate soufflé, it's been fun talking about it. Like talking about painting, even though you never take up a brush yourself."

Isobel gave a smile that had something of the cat in it. "You're flattering yourself a little, aren't you?" she said mockingly.

When Dev came home, he made straight for the shower, and Isobel looking cool and beautiful waited for him on the veranda where they usually sat. Rennie happened to be passing through the sitting room when he reappeared, and she could hardly keep her eyes off him in his clean white shirt, his thick hair still damp and looking for once darker than his face.

"You'd like some coffee, I suppose," Isobel greeted him. "Rennald, you make such gorgeous coffee do your stuff, will you?"

Rennie, who was not taking orders from Isobel, looked a moment at Dev. No smile for her, just a serious look.

"I'm going to settle for a long glass of cold beer. Isobel?"

She shook her head with a slight grimace. "I'm not a beer drinker, thanks. Not thirsty, anyway."

"Rennie?" The blue eyes had a mocking light in them, and Rennie thought furiously, "How dare he invite me in that way!" She certainly wasn't going to make it a threesome a second admirer to pander to his vanity—no matter how amusing he might find it to call her Rennie in that beguiling way.

She said with a bright ingenuous smile, "No, thanks, you can't tempt *me*," and was gone before he could think that out. If he bothered.

She brought the beer in on a tray and made herself scarce, though she did not go to join Grace and Nina in the sitting room. She switched on the lamp on the veranda near her room, took her writing pad on her knees and started a letter to her sister Anita. But the moths bothered her, as did the fact that Anita was not going to be particularly entertained by a recital of the happenings at the muster camp. And anyhow, she didn't really want to write about it.

She became aware that she was sitting tensely doing absolutely nothing. She could hear the murmur of voices, then a chair grated across the veranda floorboards and Dev's voice came clearly. "Come and I'll show you a map, Isobel." A pause, footsteps, and Dev again, but closer this time. "You might like to trace out the routes the old overlanders used to travel with their cattle long ago. Sometimes hundreds of miles, maybe almost halfway across the continent. Sometimes they were lucky and found water all the way, sometimes they lost the whole herd in a dust storm or a drought, and all but died themselves. It's a different story now the government's put down bores and watering places all along the stock routes. . . . I'll show you some of the places where there used to be cattle stations, sheep stations, homesteads. Now there's nothing but desert and ruins half buried in the sand.''

While he was speaking, they walked right past Rennie and neither of them even looked at her. She sat there when they had moved out of sight in the direction of the office, thinking of what Dev had said, thinking, *On a map! She's going to see it all on a map! Isn't she going to ask how she can get there and actually see the old tracks the overlanders used to travel? Feel the heat, cross the deserts? Find an old haunted, deserted, empty homestead, red sand piled up against its crumbling walls, wonder about the people who lived there, the women, the children, the man who failed to master the country. Oh, if it were me, I'd—*

She stopped abruptly. It was not her, it was Isobel. Then she tossed down her writing pad and went to lean on the veranda railing and look out at the night. She felt the touch of the warm air on her throat and smelled the oleanders, the roses, the last of the orange blossom. It was a long while before she moved and then she thought restlessly, where are they now? Still in the office? Still looking at maps and talking about stock routes and cattle? It was hardly likely. Perhaps Dev was asking Isobel what she thought about living here, and she was saying she would be happier at Silver Springs.

Oh, stop it, she told herself, ashamed of this fixation she had. She decided to go to bed, to forget about Dev and Isobel. But as she walked along the veranda she heard them coming in from the garden. She heard Isobel saying, "Sometimes I think you're as indifferent and as heartless as your land, Dev Deveraux."

Dev laughed. "Do you think so, Isobel? Well, to prove that I'm not, that I think about you—"

Rennie closed her ears and walked on quickly. She could imagine too well the sequel to that. . . .

The next day was Sunday and Dev was around the homestead all day. In the afternoon, he decided to take Isobel down to the swimming hole. Grace had settled down with a book, to digest her lovely dinner in peace, Nina was dozing and Rennie didn't know what to do with herself to get out of the way.

"Coming, Rennald?" Dev asked her, when he and Isobel had made their arrangements.

"No thanks," she said shortly. "I'll just mess around on my own."

He looked at her quizzically, a little disapprovingly.

"Independent?"

"I always was. I'm perfectly capable of entertaining myself."

"Well, keep your two feet on the ground and don't go hunting up any ghosts, either," he said, the blueness of his eyes flicking over the scar on her cheek.

"Ghosts?" queried Isobel, her smile distinctly chilly. "Don't tell me that Rennald claims to have seen a ghost out here."

Rennie flushed at her tone, which seemed to imply that she was merely trying to make herself interesting. Before she could think it through, she had retorted, "You'd be surprised if you knew whose ghost I saw in the mirror of the Silver Springs drawing room!"

Dev's eyes narrowed. If Isobel was showing obvious skepticism, he was certainly not, and Rennie flushed guiltily. It would put her in a spot if he insisted that she talk about her experience. She could not possibly tell the truth. To her relief, Dev merely said, "Very interesting, I'm sure, Rennald. You must tell us all about it some time." Then he put his hand on Isobel's arm, sent Rennie a narrow look and moved off. She gave a sigh of relief.

She put on her jeans and went out to the saddling yard. Soon she was riding madly out over the red sands and in among the mulgas with their feathery downlike hanging leaves, where the shadows were fantastically painted in cobalt and indigo.

CHAPTER SEVEN

SHE COULD HEAR SOMEONE whistling "The Dying Stock-man", the notes clear and sharp and gay on the hot, still air. "Jake," she thought, with a curious feeling she couldn't quite analyze. Part dread, part anticipation. She rather more than suspected that he must have been riding over to the homestead in search of her. Well, there was no point in trying to avoid the unavoidable, and she had promised him that they would talk again. It was something that he got some pleasure out of her company. And surely he would watch it this time and not make a pass at her.

"Hello, Renniebird," he greeted her. He was spruced up today, his boots shining, his checked shirt clean. And his eyes looked the color of spring leaves in the sunlight though far from as innocent. They looked incongruously like jewels in that dark face of his. "I was hoping I'd find you somewhere around, seeing that our tomorrow didn't come at the muster. What happened? I can't believe you asked to be taken home."

Rennie, riding beside him now, shook her head. "Mr. Deveraux found me and Isobel too much bother to have around while there was so much work to be done. He packed us off back to the homestead. Didn't he tell you?"

"Not a word. Why should he? He's my boss, not my mate," he said dryly. "I've never been invited to take part in the social life at the homestead. Outside's the place for me, and in fact it looks as if I've stepped out of line by trying to fraternize with the cook. Which brings me to a question I wanted to ask. What exactly are you? Are you the cook? Or are you, as he said that day down by the water hole, his guest?''

Rennie colored. ''Isobel Sandison and her aunt are his guests. I'm here because I make a good job of the cooking.''

''So. All the same, he was telling me to lay off. Does he have a soft spot for you? Or does he feel responsible, considering my reputation great with the cattle and horses, rotten with women.''

''I wouldn't know,'' said Rennie uncomfortably. ''But I hardly think he has a soft spot for me. I'm not to his liking at all—he finds fault with me every which way. I'm always in trouble.''

He grinned at her. ''Do you mind?''

She raised her eyebrows. ''Why should I?''

''Most girls would. In fact, all the females who come to Nimmitibel, though I'll admit there aren't many, seem to set their caps for my boss.''

''I'm different,'' said Rennie stoically. And wished forlornly that she was.

They rode in silence through a thick belt of trees, then came to a little clearing where there was water.

''No good for a swim,'' said Jake. ''But pretty, isn't it?''

Rennie nodded. Her eyes delighted in the feathery leaves, the blue shadows, the stillness of the water. There were a few wild fuchsias blooming, an unexpected patch of yellow everlastings and some small blue-capped birds flitting about in the trees. They left their horses and by mutual consent walked down to the sloping bank above the water. It was burningly, exhaustingly hot, and Rennie felt fit for nothing but to throw herself down on the ground and pass into a mindless state. It was too hot for sleep. She had never felt quite like this before, but this day was hotter than any they had experienced, and it made her think of the early explorers and marvel that they had ever been able to go on and accomplish all they had.

"How do you keep going when it's summer and there's work to be done?" she asked Jake.

He shrugged. "I'm from Broken Hill," he said, as if that explained a lot. He took the heat completely for granted the heat and the dust and the flies and the sweat. It wasn't drawing-room stuff, not the sort of thing you wrote home about. Not pretty and romantic. And yet it was the sort of thing you could learn to accept. So long as you didn't imagine you could keep on looking fresh as an ad for cologne, thought Rennie, smiling a little at the thought.

She and Jake lay back on the red earth with its covering of needle-fine leaves. Sometimes they talked and sometimes they didn't, and always Rennie saw Dev's face whenever she closed her eyes—and wished she didn't. She felt reasonably sure that Jake would keep his promise and not lay a hand on her today, and if she felt a little edgy it was not on his account. She answered without self-consciousness when he asked her presently about her family. She told him about her three older sisters and how her mother had wanted a boy.

"And I arrived. She called me Rennald because that was her maiden name and she'd have called a son that. Maybe the fact that I've always been a bit of a problem has something to do with that. I don't know. I've never done the things that were expected of me and I always seemed to have everyone worried sick about what I'd do next trying to find my niche in life. The others are all married, but I seem to keep falling in love with the wrong man the one who is tied up already." She stopped abruptly, for she realized it had happened again, and this time it was different. It was real.

Jake looked across at her, his hard green eyes enigmatic, fathomless. "If you've fallen for me, Renniebird, in your quiet way, then you've done it again," he said after a moment. "Did you by any chance mean that?"

"No," she said, carefully casual and undramatic. "I'm not even vaguely interested in falling in love out here—"

"Out here? You mean, in the unspeakable Outback?"

"Of course I don't! I like it here—"

"Well then." He lit a cigarette, blew out the match and flipped it away. He was lying on his side, leaning on one elbow and squinting at her in the sunlight that fell through the trees. "Pity I'm not in a position to offer you something permanent. The whole thing would blow up if I tried to get you to come to bed with me, I suppose."

"It would," said Rennie firmly, coloring despite a determination to appear wordly-wise. Then she added with a sudden flash of irritation, "Why do you have to say such things? And to look at me like that? That's not really keeping your promise. As far as I'm concerned, things are fine the way they are now, except that I hate the way you're talking and I don't understand what you're trying to do—to tease me or provoke me or—or dare me."

"Maybe the last. I thought you were the sort of girl who would accept a dare. And I'm not what anyone would call gallant." He rolled over on his back and closed his eyes. His mouth was bitter. "Okay, I'll stay where I belong—right on the other side of the dingo fence."

"I don't know what you mean by that, either," she flared.

"No? Well, I won't bother to explain." He said nothing more at all, and she was aware of an irritating sense of guilt and wondered if he had aroused that deliberately. He was subtle in some ways.

Near sundown, the Major Mitchell cockatoos came flying down to drink at the water, and Rennie scrambled to her feet. Her hair was mussed and her neck felt sticky with perspiration and mentally she felt wrung out. Jake seemed to have that effect on her. She stood looking down at him. He had opened his eyes and was watching her.

"I'll have to go. I've a meal to prepare."

"Sunday evenings, too?"

"Every evening."

He got up and his eyes raked her over. "If I touch you you'll yell, won't you?" he asked conversationally. "Well, I don't know who'd hear you, but I suppose you're entitled to your glass case. Someone's going to break it sometime, though." He smiled at her strangely, and she stood irresolutely, not knowing what to expect of him, the color bright in her cheeks. He took a single step toward her, ready to break his promise, and then Dev Deveraux appeared through the trees leading his black horse.

Rennie, who hadn't known she was holding her breath, breathed again. She knew how guilty she must appear, flushed and disheveled as she was. She knew what Dev must think and she hated herself. She wished she could say something glib and flippantlike, "Are you hungry, Mr. Deveraux? Do you want me to go home and cook your dinner?" but she couldn't utter a word.

It was Jake who spoke, his lips twisting. "She's coming boss." Then he strode off, threw himself onto his horse and rode away.

Rennie's voice returned and she said stupidly,

"You're very clever the way you hunt me down, Mr. Deveraux. How do you manage it?"

"I hope you appreciate my cleverness," he said shortly. "Fortunately I saw your horse. . . . And now seems a good time to tell you. I'm flying over to Silver Springs tomorrow to check up on the fats that Tim is cutting out for the saleyards."

Rennie raised her eyebrows. "What's that got to do with me?"

He gave a grim smile. "I'm not inviting you to do another bit of skydiving," he said curtly. "I'm telling you because I plan to make it a general exodus. Miss Sandison can't take heat like we've had here today, and for various reasons it's time Grace moved. Isobel needs a break her endurance has been tested enough, besides which she wants to hunt up your ghost, to add a touch of spice to her stories." He paused and gave her a searching look and she colored faintly.

But her awkwardness about the ghost was wiped out by another thought. Of course she was to leave Nimmitibel, too, and of course she would be left at Silver Springs, and that would be the end of—what? She was not thinking of her peculiar association with Jake Ridley. She was thinking of this man who stood near her, and she felt with a sense of desolation that she had no more control over her life than a fish or a bird or an insect had. If she was prey then she was prey. There was absolutely nothing she could do. You couldn't throw yourself on a man's mercy and tell him that you were—

"Are you going to tell me about your ghost, Rennald Baxter?" he asked unexpectedly.

Rennie shrugged, suddenly weary of this talk of ghosts. All that had happened that evening at Silver Springs was that she had picked up a mental image of Isobel Sandison, who had discovered that Nimmitibel didn't come up to her expectations and wished she were back where she had first met Dev. He had explained such phenomena that way himself.

She said flatly, "I don't believe in ghosts. I was only fooling."

His look darkened, his brows descended. "You're intent on being a stranger to me, aren't you—keeping me at arms' length?"

"What else should I be or do? I'm the cook." She swung up into the saddle and a minute later had raced off ahead of him.

Dev served up another dose of history that night for Isobel. It seemed she had been neglecting her articles and that time was running short. He talked about the intrepid explorers, Burke and Wills, of the settlers who had come after and been defeated, of the Wild, untamed, untamable land. And Rennie listened fascinated.

"Here on Nimmitibel nature will accept us if we don't intrude beyond her sanctions—if we are gentle with her and go along with her ways." He paced slowly along the veranda looking out beyond her garden to the far horizons and the hot starry night, and Isobels's pen flew dutifully across the clean white page, leaving a trail of shorthand notes. He had paused and she looked up expectantly. But Dev was looking at Rennie now, bemused, like a man in a dream, and for an infinitesmal second, Rennie seemed to see right inside his mind. She saw his red lands spread out under the burning sun, his cattle by the water holes and the feed so vigilantly supervised. She saw a man on a black horse and a girl at his side, and the girl was Rennald Baxter. Rennie blinked hard. Her musings showed just exactly how she was deluding herself. The girl would be Isobel, but of course she was imagining the whole thing—she couldn't possibly see inside Dev's mind. Now his eyes had left her face, and she was sure they had not seen her at all. He continued to talk, and Isobel was taking notes again.

Rennie got up and moved along the veranda to stand there by herself and to hate herself for falling in love with Dev Deveraux— another man who was already tied up.

The next morning they left for Siver Springs—Rennie, Isobel, Nina and Grace, all in Grace's car. Dev was to fly down in the afternoon in the Cessna. Isobel wouldn't go with him: she didn't like small planes. And Rennie wasn't asked.

She had a feeling that her Outback adventure was over, that it had begun and ended as illogically as one of those spiraling twisters that danced over the red plains on hot still days. In no time at all there would be nothing of it left, nothing to remember.

Which was desperately untrue. It was going to take her a long time to forget.

I'M AFRAID YOU'VE MISSED NANCY,'' Meg told Dr. Grace almost the minute they set foot in the house. And how cool and beautiful it seemed after the rigors of Nimmitibel! Rennie hadn't realized before what a difference there was. She saw the incredulous relief in Nina Sandison's face and a sort of hungry calculating pleasure in Isobel's eyes. "Tim takes her along with him all the time now. They're getting on like a house on fire, and I'm afraid you'll have a hard job persuading her to go back to Adelaide, Dr. Grace.''

There was just sufficient archness in Meg's tone for her meaning to be quite plain. Tim and Nancy, she implied, were falling in love, and it was serious. But Grace was not impressed. She marched purposefully across the veranda and opened the wire screen door as if she were going into her own house.

"No doubt a very wise stratagem on your son's part,

Meg," she said offhandedly. "But Nancy's barely out of school. Of course she wants to try her wings. . . . And now, could we have some lunch?"

Meg had set the table on the veranda where the light fell soft and green through a screen of passion-fruit vines. As she brought the salad and placed it on the table, she asked with a pretence at casualness, "Has Dev said anything about coming back to live at Silver Springs?"

Instead of answering, Grace looked at Isobel, who merely shrugged and said coolly, "Don't ask me to discuss Dev's business," and got on with her salad.

An obvious snub. And she had already greeted Meg in a patronizing way. Rennie had noticed that and had kissed Meg affectionately on both cheeks to make up for it.

Lunch over, Meg suggested that the two girls might like to ride out and look for Tim and Nancy. "It should be pleasant today among the trees, not too hot."

"Not after Nimmitibel," agreed Grace, standing on the veranda smoking a cigarillo while Nina lay on the cane lounge behind her. Rennie didn't see that there would be all that much difference in the outside temperature, but later, as she and Isobel rode across the paddock, she realized that harsh though it was, this was a softer countryside than that at Nimmitibel. It was easier on the eye, there were miles of gray green saltbush and patches of grass, providing relief from the starkness of red sand.

She and Isobel didn't speak to each other. They let their horses amble along rather aimlessly, and it was Rennie who got down to open the gate that led into the paddock where the fats had been mustered and yarded, ready for Dev's inspection. Isobel followed her through, and Rennie, looking at the stock, remarked that they were beautiful beasts, in prime condition, their coats glossy and sleek.

"They should fetch a good price, wouldn't you think?"

Isobel gave her a contemptuous look.

"Do you think you know the least little thing about cattle just because you tagged along on a horse one day at the muster? I suppose when you go back to England or wherever you happen to be going, you'll bore everyone stiff with all your stories of the Outback and forget to tell them that you were the cook."

They stared at each other and sparks of fire flared up in Rennie's eyes.

"At least I managed to stay perpendicular, while you were flat on your back in a bath of perspiration."

"Because you're tough," retorted Isobel. "And you look it! You'll make an ideal mate for that barbarous and unnaturally good-looking stockman of Dev's. I'm quite sure you won't in the least mind sleeping out on the ground with him instead of in a decent house. Thank heavens I have a little more breeding and sensitivity!"

"Maybe you have just a little too much."

"By that you mean—exactly what?"

"That you don't belong in the uncivilized Outback," said Rennie unwisely.

"Silver Springs is civilized," snapped Isobel. "And I mean to—" She suddenly clamped down and said nothing more.

"Silver Springs is where the Langs belong. It's not Dev's home."

"Of course you would side with the Langs," said the other girl acidly. "Though nobody cares in the least what you think, believe me. Dev won't ask your opinion when he wants to make a decision."

"I wouldn't dream of offering it," said Rennie spiritedly. "I think it's entirely up to Dev."

"And his wife," said Isobel.

Rennie felt a strange shock in her heart, even though she had known all along that this was going to happen. She said constrainedly, "You are going to marry him, then? You don't want to go back to Adelaide to your friends there?"

Isobel stared at her. "You'd like the field to yourself, wouldn't you? Then you'd aim higher than the head stockman. Don't imagine I'm not aware that you've been doing everyting you can think of to fascinate Dev Deveraux, beginning with your ridiculous jump from his Cessna. It's a wonder you didn't break your neck. And that's exactly what you will do one of these days if you persist in stupid displays of recklessness. And now fooling around with some stockman—do you imagine you'll make Dev jealous? He's more likely to worry that you'll get yourself into the most elementary kind of trouble."

Rennie stared at her. That last gibe was really insulting. Suddenly she decided to waste no more time on Isobel. She turned her horse's head and galloped back toward the gate, leaving Isobel to please herself.

They didn't meet up again during the afternoon. Rennie had no idea what Isobel did or where she went, but she rode down to the river, which just now was little more than a series of potholes. She followed it idly along and didn't see a sign of Nancy or Tim. She heard the Cessna coming over and shaded her eyes, watching it come down. She wasn't anywhere near the landing strip, and that was all to the good because she didn't want to be around to welcome Dev. Nancy and Tim, and doubtless Isobel, would do that.

She took her time about going back to the homestead. Dev would have gone out to look over the fats and probably he would stay the night at the homestead. So it could be the last she would see of him. She wondered if Grace would try to force the issue now, refuse to sign on

Tim Lang as manager and demand that Dev take over. On what grounds, Rennie wondered. It seemed to her that the deciding vote was now Isobel's, so there was not very much doubt about what was going to happen.

It was sundown when she reached the saddling yards. The sky was dramatic. There were great clouds flat on the horizon and the scene was fantastically beautiful. But not as beautiful as it would be at Nimmitibel, she thought. She climbed the steps to the veranda to find everyone there but Isobel, who, as it happened arrived about the same time, stepping through the door from the house looking beautiful and cool, even hostessy, in a silver blue dress, her blond hair shining and newly washed.

Dev's blue eyes flicked across to Rennie and he nodded at her rather curtly but didn't speak. In fact, a silence seemed to have fallen all around, a rather tense silence. Isobel crossed over and stood next to Dev, her back against the railing, and Nancy said with a sort of determined brightness, "Hi, Rennie. I looked out for you this afternoon. Where did you get to?" She was not her usual self, and Tim, arms folded across his chest, barely managed a smile.

What had caused everyone to look so odd? *It's not me,* thought Rennie. And it was not Isobel who had just appeared. She looked around at the faces of the small gathering wondering what had happened.

Grace alone appeared unconcerned, while Meg looked as if she might burst into tears at any minute, her face flushed with the strain of controlled emotion.

Isobel voiced Rennie's thoughts.

"What's the matter with everyone? What happened? I was brushing out my hair and I heard such an uproar I thought you'd all gone crazy."

"It's a little matter of carelessness," said Dev coolly, after a second. "The herd of fats I came all this way to inspect have somehow or other disappeared. I've wasted my time.''

Rennie stared. ''But '' she began.

Isobel interpolated quickly, ''I'm afraid I'm completely in the dark. I haven't seen the precious fats.''

What a lie! Rennie could hardly believe her ears, and Isobel was looking at her as if she dared her to contradict.

Dev was watching Tim, his eyebrows raised. The younger man said emphatically, ''I'm willing to swear to you I had those fats cut out from the herd the men were mustering over the past week. Nancy—any one of the men—will confirm that.''

''I don't question it,'' said Dev. He moved a little. ''But you didn't find it worth a bit of time to check that the gates were closed. Someone slipped up, and the blame rests with you. You check up on your team, even if it's hellishly hot, and you miss out on half an hour—or half a day—of your personal life. You've been too taken up with entertaining my young cousin. I thought you'd have come out to the airstrip to meet me instead of letting me bring the jeep in on my own. And it's no good telling me you thought that Isobel would come out, that's hardly the point.'' He paused and finished heavily, ''You start getting lax, careless, and it goes on from there.''

Rennie saw the whole picture with a vivid awareness. Of course those gates had been closed. She had opened them herself. She hadn't shut them when she rode off. Neither, it seemed, had Isobel. And it seemed extremely likely that Isobel's omission had been deliberate, so that Tim would be in trouble. It would suit her purpose best if Dev should decide without her intervention to take over Silver Springs. Well, she was not going to get away with it. Rennie took a deep breath and said carefully, ''I went to look at those fats. And I . . . I forgot to close the gates. I'm sorry.''

There was silence, and they all looked at her. In Isobel's eyes were such icy daggers that it was a wonder Rennie didn't fall down dead. Dev stared at her, at first incredulously, then furiously, then narrowly.

"My God *you*!" he said below his breath. "You are a little troublemaker, aren't you? Everywhere you go. . . . Is this true?" She nodded, clenching her fists. "Do you know what you've done? You've wiped out a week's hard work. Those beasts will be all over the place now. It will mean a complete remuster of the south-gate paddock. And I've wasted my time coming here. . . . My apologies, Tim. It's simply another result of allowing women around the ranch." He moved abruptly. He looked fed up with the whole bunch of them. Rennie would not have been in the least surprised if he had turned on his heel, driven back to the Cessna and disappeared into the sky. But of course he could not do that. And she was the woman he was referring to. Isobel had to be considered, and Isobel was innocent, blameless. "Well, we can break it up now that we have the facts," he said curtly.

Grace, cheated of her triumph, looked at him belligerently. "All the same, Dev, I'm going to have a word with you - privately about the business that brought me here."

"Privately?" His dark brows came down and he looked like thunder. "Doesn't everybody know why you're here—to find fault with Tim? You thought you'd found it today, now Rennie here has claimed she's the one who's done the mischief. I haven't changed my mind about my manager. Moreover," he added, "if you hold your peace it looks like you might yet see the family reinstated at Silver Springs."

"I think not," said Grace coolly.

Everyone knew what was being discussed except, it

seemed, Nancy and Tim. Tim had relaxed, and Rennie thought, *He must hate me.* She didn't dare look at Isobel.

Nancy said happily, "I knew it wasn't Tim. He *is* conscientious. I knew all the gates were closed." She looked at Rennie regretfully. "I'm glad you were brave enough to own up, though I can't see how it happened. It's just so elementary."

Rennie knew how it had happened. It had been deliberate. She could only marvel at such underhanded, mean tactics. Didn't Isobel have the courage to tell Dev how she felt about Nimmitibel? Didn't she know that for her, he would pack up just like that and come back to Silver Springs? At least that way Tim would have an honorable discharge, and Rennie felt certain that Dev would see he got another equally good job.

She wondered what everyone would have to say to her about her apparent stupidity, but no one, now that Nancy had said her piece, had a thing to say. Except, of course, Dev. And he got her to himself after dinner with a "please explain."

"You've never struck me as being—" he stopped and searched his mind "—a particularly brainless sort of a girl. And so I'd like to hear the full story of your slipup. Come along now, all of it." His voice was brisk, his eyes hard, and there was no escape. Rennie bit her lip, looked wildly away from him into the garden where the half moon, a silver globe hidden behind a dark disc, hung three-dimentionally in the sky.

"I've said I'm sorry. Isn't that enough?"

"No, it's not. Why did you go out to the yards in the first place?"

"Well, I didn't have any plan at all. I went out for a ride. I couldn't see Nancy and Tim, and I went through this gate and saw the cattle yarded there. I stood and looked at them for a while. The sun was hot on their hides, all shining and beautiful." She stopped and looked at him briefly. His eyes were not on her but on the tip of his cigarette, and his mouth was set in a line of hardness.

"You were alone?"

She swallowed and told a direct lie. "Yes." She finished hopelessly, "I just forgot about the gate when I rode off."

Now he looked up at her and there was a grim smile on his lips. "Haven't you forgotten something? Or do you think I'm so completely gullible that this—forgetting business is going to take me in? I want to know why you opened the holding-yard gates."

Rennie felt her face pale. She had completely forgotten that the cattle would have had to be released from the holding yard. She didn't know how to explain that away. But she was saved the trouble. Dev did the explaining for her.

"You want me to come to Silver Springs, don't you? You'd like to see Jake Ridley in charge out there at Nimmitibel." He tossed his cigarette out into the night in a flying arc. His voice was savage. "Well, that will never happen—never in a million years. So wake up from your schoolgirl dream and make up your mind to it." He took two strides toward her and stood glowering down at her with eyes that were darkly furious. Her lips parted in fright, and she was not in the least surprised when he gripped her by the arms and shook her—hard. She stared at him wide-eyed, pale-cheeked, and suddenly he let her go. She saw his fists clench and heard him grit out with a kind of weariness, "We'll see what's to be done with you tomorrow."

WHEN SHE WENT TO BED later on, she couldn't sleep for thinking of those words. She felt as apprehensive as if her very life were at stake. And in a way, she thought wearily as she tossed and turned in her comfortable bed, it was because it seemed so very probable that the brief time she had known Dev Deveraux was nearly at its end, and she could think of nothing but him. She knew with certainty that he was the one man in the world she could love until death devotedly, loyally, no matter what he should ask of her, where he should take her.

There were tears on her lashes when she slept.

She felt completely wrung out in the morning. She got up to a quiet household. Nina was still asleep in the luxury of a pretty bedroom equipped with its own bathroom. Isobel had not yet appeared, and Tim and Nancy were out on the ranch with the work of remustering to be done. Grace, for some reason, had breakfasted early and was preparing to go out in her car and she didn't offer to take anyone along with her. There was only Meg to join Rennie when she fetched herself toast and coffee from the kitchen and took it to the breakfast table on the veranda. She didn't dare ask where Dev was, and the thought that he might already have gone back to Nimmitibel was a dismal one.

Meg remarked after a moment, "I'm sorry you opened that gate, Rennie, but I suppose not being a country girl you didn't understand the importance of these things. One simply never leaves a gate open. Never. And certainly one never opens yard gates on stock that have been mustered for any purpose whatever." There was distinct reproof in her tone, and it irked Rennie that she must listen and make no protest. Meg must think she was stupid. Dev at least had decided that she had acted deliberately, though it troubled her to think he imagined she was foolishly in love with Jake. Her little lecture over,

Meg disappeared. Rennie finished her coffee and had picked up her dishes to take them to the kitchen when Isobel came out, beautifully cool and poised and without the least sign of embarrassment about what had happened the day before. She tossed a large envelope down on the table.

"What's all this about a ghost at Silver Springs? No one seems to know a thing about it."

Rennie shrugged. "I don't have any story to tell you. But I'm sure you can make one up yourself," she added unkindly.

Isobel sent her a contemptuous look from her pale blue eyes. "Just as I thought. I had a feeling you'd just been spinning some tale to Dev in an effort to enlarge your ego, so I sealed my letter to my boss." She stopped dead, her pupils dilating, then she blinked quickly and managed a smile. Dev had come from somewhere outside and was mounting the veranda steps.

"Good morning." His voice was hard, and he stood broad and handsome, his eyes dazzlingly blue, the sunlight touching the tips of his lashes to gold. He told Isobel, "I'm flying the Cessna home this morning. Do you want to come, or have you had your fill of all my place has to offer?"

"I'd like to come," said Isobel after an instant. Rennie, knowing her dislike of small planes, knew she had hesitated on that account. She thought it a little unkind of Dev to offer no alternative.

"Right." His eyes went to the letter on the table. "A letter to your boss? Leave it here—it can go with the mail this afternoon. . . . Now go along and pack, will you? We'll take off when you're ready."

And now for me, thought Rennie with dread in her heart, when Isobel had disappeared, looking not altogether pleased. Dev was not in the best of moods, it was obvious. Was she, too, to go with the mail in the afternoon?

She jumped a little when he said, "In a moment, you can go and get packed up too."

She felt herself pale. "To go with—with the mail?" she asked faintly.

"What?"

She drew a deep breath. "I presume that would be the quickest and easiest way to get rid of me."

He stood frowning down at her, and she hardly dared to look at him, because she knew that her eyes would be hungry, betraying. Her hand strayed absently to the scar on her cheek, and he said roughly, "Forget that—it's like a beauty spot on a flawless skin." He made an abrupt movement, turned half away from her. "Do you—*want* to go?"

She said, "No," before she had realized.

"Just as I suspected. Well then, you might be pleased to know you are to come to Nimmitibel in the Cessna, too."

She stared at him stupefied, unbelieving, and then her heart began to pound with joy. An idiotic reasonless joy. Because it would be far wiser to make a clean break now, to cease torturing herself—

"Obviously I can't take Isobel back on her own," he explained, dampening her joy. "And it would be cruel to demand that her aunt return to the hardship of Nimmitibel now that she has discovered what Silver Springs can offer."

"I understand," said Rennie bitterly. "And of course, I can make life happier with my cooking—"

"You can," he agreed. There was a pause. They looked at each other.

"And I will see Jake again," said Rennie.

A cynical gleam appeared in the blueness of his eyes.

"You're certainly making a happy man of my head stockman," he said frigidly. "However, you'd be wise to get over your infatuation. I've warned you not to fool around with him."

Rennie's eyebrows went up. "I'm not in the habit of fooling around with men, as you put it. It so happens I like Jake—very much."

"Do you indeed? Well, that's a cozy way of putting it." She was held by his eyes, could not look away and wished that she could. Yet to look away would be some kind of surrender—a backing down. And she would never surrender to Dev Deveraux. He said slowly, deliberately, "I think it's time you knew that Jake Ridley already has a wife."

Rennie felt a small flash of triumph. "That's not news to me. I've known for some time."

"And it doesn't matter to you?"

"In that his marriage was not a happy one, it matters. But how else should it matter, Mr. Deveraux?"

There was a long pause. Then he said, "God knows," sounding completely weary. "You are—what? Twenty-one or so? I suppose I can give you roughly fifteen years. In my world, such things matter. But not, I take it, in yours."

"She's left him, hasn't she?" asked Rennie. "He hasn't seen her for years."

"And so you regard him as being—free?"

"You think no girl should associate with a man in Jay's unenviable position?" she countered.

"Not the way you're doing. However, it would seem we have different ideas."

"I'm sure we do," said Rennie tightly.

He lit a cigarette without offering her one, leaned back against the veranda rail and looked at her through smoke and half-closed eyes.

"I wonder about you, Rennald Baxter. You're remote, delicate, dreamy—but just what goes on in that shining head of yours I can't fathom. You'll drop down from the sky on the end of a parachute, watch a man castrate a scrub bull, stand in the flying dust while the cattle rush—all with never a thought of danger. And now—am I wrong, or are you insinuating that you'd live with a man who already has a wife somewhere or other?"

Rennie bit hard on her lip. What was the answer to that one? Suppose the man was Dev Deveraux? She said confusedly, "If one loves, one will do anything."

"One would have to be very sure indeed that one loved," he said dryly. "Do you?"

His eyes were intent on hers, and suddenly she had to look away.

She said carefully, "I don't like this conversation, Mr. Deveraux."

"In other words, I'm to mind my own business."

The conversation ended flatly, just like that. The next moment he simply walked away.

Rennie went to her room to pack.

CHAPTER EIGHT

THEY FLEW OUT to Nimmitibel late in the morning. Isobel hated every second of the short flight, but Rennie felt invigorated, elated, despite the fact that the pilot, Dev, was almost completely silent.

She thought it was going to be a strange sojourn at Nimmitibel now, with Grace and Nina Sandison back at Silver Springs and only herself and Isobel and Dev there apart, of course, from Ettie and the aboriginal girls who didn't in any case live in the homestead. Strange and intimidating, too; she was quite sure she had been made to come. It all had to end sometime, somehow when Dev and Isobel had sorted themselves out.

Meanwhile, she would see Jake again. That was inevitable. And the next day, when she had finished in the kitchen, she went out riding on her own. As if it had been preordained, she saw Jake Ridley down by the water hole. Isobel had gone out in the jeep with Dev, and Rennie had not been invited. Nor would she have gone if she had been.

Seeing Jake was somehow spiced with danger, and she didn't altogether enjoy it. Yet she believed that she could help him, even if she was not making him the happy man that Dev had suggested, simply by being her natural self, by being companionable rather than provocative, by encouraging him to talk about his work, his country and, if he wanted, his life.

But his life, she discovered, was not going to be laid bare to her. And she had to work constantly to persuade him to keep their relationship impersonal. Despite the promise he had made her, he persisted that evening in attempting to embrace her, to kiss her, and she had to be really adroit to avoid him.

She was exhausted when she got back to the homestead, and by the time she had prepared dinner, she was almost too tired to eat it and wanted nothing more than to shower, fall into bed and sleep.

She met Jake several times after that, and it didn't strike her that he must be taking time off from work until Dev tackled her.

"Where are you off to, Rennald?" he wanted to know one afternoon as she came through to the veranda where he was waiting for Isobel.

"For a ride," said Rennie with a touch of defiance.

He gave her a searching look. "Meeting Jake Ridley?"

"It's hardly your concern."

"It's my concern in one way, and I think even you must agree. He has a job to do and he's meant to be doing it."

She flushed to the roots of her hair, and he continued darkly, "I didn't bring you back to Nimmitibel so that you could go straight into the arms of my head stockman, Rennald Baxter. In fact, I sometimes ask myself why in hell I *did* bring you back again."

"To do the cooking," she said tartly. "And to chaperone Isobel. Though I can't say I've been attending to the second part of my duties very well—it's not up to me to watch how you behave yourself when you take her out in the afternoons." She could see sparks of anger burning in his eyes, but she continued determinedly. "Nor is it up to you to be concerned with what Jake and I do—after he's knocked off work," she added.

A muscle tightened in his jaw. "I can make a pretty educated guess about that, just the same," he said below his breath. "Would you like to hear?"

"No thank you," she said quickly, and began to go down the steps. "Because I assure you you'd be quite wrong." She began to walk quickly along the path and his voice followed her.

"If you're telling me the truth, that's all I want to know."

She felt uneasy about Jake that afternoon, because of course he found her, even though she didn't go to the water hole, but rode instead out through the mulga until she found a thick grove of trees above the riverbed where there was a considerable pool. She had dismounted from the horse and was wandering along the river bank when he came.

"Hi, Renniebird. You led me a dance this afternoon. I thought you must have been given orders to stay home."

She looked at him worriedly. "You should be at work, shouldn't you? I've been accused of dragging you away from it."

"Well, the accusation's a fair one, isn't it?" He had come close and stood looking down into her face.

"Of course it's not," she exclaimed indignantly.

He smiled a little, and she had a glimpse of teeth almost as white as Dev's but not as even. "You can't keep away from me any more than I can keep away from you."

She stared at him. Was that how he saw it? And why on earth hadn't it struck her before that Dev's being free in the afternoons didn't mean that Jake Ridley should be free, too? In fact, on the contrary . . . . She said carefully,

"Well, it can't go on. I won't come out riding anymore, so it will be no use your looking for me."

"You'll have to meet me at night, then."

"Perhaps," said Rennie.

"Perhaps? What does that mean?" Suddenly his body was against hers and his arms were around her locking her against him.

"Let me go!" she breathed, twisting her head aside to avoid his mouth. She gritted her teeth and somehow got her hands against his chest and pushed with all her strength, at the same time kicking out at him with one booted foot. Free, she stood facing him with fear and hostility, breathing hard. The sky above had turned a brilliant scarlet, the pool in the riverbed was streaked with red and silver and the birds coming screaming down to drink filled the air with their floating bodies, white and pink and gray, until the uproar and disturbance around them seemed to match exactly Rennie's inner turmoil.

She told Jake, perspiration running down her neck, her cheeks flushed, her hair falling around her face, "You sizzle all over me. You spoil everything between us"

"Everything between us? What's between us? Do you call words anything? You fight like a hellcat if I so much as lay a finger on you, so what is there between us for me to spoil?"

"Companionship," said Rennie. "Isn't that something? Must it all come back to sex? How can I even try to be friends with you when promises mean nothing to you, when you . . . when you behave like a savage?"

He turned aside, lit one of his cigarettes, then looked at her with eyes that were stone hard.

"Like a savage," he repeated. "Is that how it seems to you? As for promises, aren't emotions more important than promises? I have only to look at you at your lips, your hair, your smooth skin, the curves of your body—and I want you. Is that ... unnatural? Is that behaving like a savage? Don't you just a little bit want my arms around you, too—''

"No," she said violently. "I'm more than flesh and blood."

He looked away from her, his eyes becoming slits. "Then if I tell you that I love you? Does that make any difference?"

She felt her heart contract. He had said that almost as though he meant it. And yet she knew that he didn't mean it, that it was no more than guile, an attempt to get his own way. She had been utterly naïve in thinking that what he needed most was a renewal of faith in the female sex, that they could be friends. Almost anyone else would have known very early in the piece that a man like Jake Ridley just wasn't interested in platonic friendships. There was exactly one thing he wanted of her, and in various ways he had told her so every time they met.

She said tiredly, "It makes no difference at all because it's not true. I think we'd better break it up. Apparently we can't be friends, and I don't enjoy fighting you off. You've admitted that promises mean nothing to you, so I think we can say goodbye, here and now. I'll be leaving the Outback soon in any case," she finished, her voice beginning to shake.

His face had twisted into a mask that destroyed entirely his devastating good looks.

"So this is the finish, is it? I've made a fool of myself over you, and you've ceased to be amused. It's been so good to know you," he went on with bitter irony, "but now it's time to say goodbye." He held out his hand to her, then withdrew it before she had time to reciprocate.

"Of course, we can't shake hands. I just might jerk you off your feet and try to seduce you."

He turned his back and walked away before she knew it had happened, and she stared after him blankly, with a feeling of insupportable failure. Somewhere in her heart she was terribly hurt for him, and yet what could she do? She simply couldn't handle him, and it seemed that her efforts to help him had done more harm than good. Yet she had pictured herself—oh, with what ludicrous ingenuousness doing so much for him. . . .

She rode slowly back to the homestead, feeling shaken and upset and very much as if she were the one who had behaved badly, and in a way, she supposed she was. She left her horse at the yards with one of the men and reached the homestead to discover that Isobel's boss, Vince Scott, had just arrived. He was a middle-aged man, a fraction overweight, worldly, charming and very much master of himself despite the obvious fact that he found the heat more than trying. He had discarded his coat and his tie and rolled up the sleeves of his white shirt, and the smart car from which he had just stepped was covered in red dust.

He kissed Isobel, said she was a wonderful girl to put herself through "all this" for the paper, shook hands with Dev heartily and with Rennie courteously. "Rennald's a sort of Jill-of-all-trades," said Isobel with unexpected lightheartedness. "She's our cook—and wow, can she cook—and she's also standing in as chaperone for poor darling Aunt Nina who's found the Outback totally abrasive."

"Chaperone?" queried Vince as they all went up the veranda steps.

"It would hardly be the thing for a bachelor like myself to ask a charming girl out here on her own," said Dev dryly.

Vince looked at Rennie with a slight smile. "So you've made it two charming girls. You cattlemen certainly do yourselves proud!" His eyes, taking in the far-from-opulent interior of the homestead as they went inside, commented silently that perhaps he had spoken too soon.

"I suppose you wouldn't say no to a glass of beer," Dev suggested. "Isobel, show your boss where he can have a wash and see if you can find a clean towel for him. He'll want to get rid of some of that dust before he sits down."

Isobel hesitated fractionally and then accepted the order, for an order it undoubtedly was. Rennie offered quickly, "I'll fetch the beer, shall I?"

"You may help me, if you like," said Dev coolly.

In the kitchen his eyes raked her over, and she knew that she looked haggard and spent and far from attractive.

"What happened to you, Rennald Baxter? You're late in. Did you get lost? That scar of yours is blazing on your cheek like a star. Funny, that. I always connect it with your heart." She said nothing, but her heart was pounding. She felt strongly that he was displeased with her, but he didn't press her to answer his question and watched for a minute while she set out glasses. "Four," he said sharply when she put three on the tray. "Dinner can wait. Don't tell me you have to get on with that yet. And if you'd rather have a brandy—and God knows you look as though that's what you need, and I very much wonder why—then have one."

"No, thank you." She didn't want to make herself different. She reminded him stiffly, "Isobel doesn't like beer—"

"Then fix a jug of ice," he said irritably. "I'll find the gin and a bottle of lime juice."

The other two were already on the veranda when they

went back through the house. Isobel had brought out the bowl of roses Rennie had arranged early in the morning and set it on the small table. She looked up at Dev with a bright smile. "Oh, good—you've remembered I don't like beer."

He took the credit and dealt with the drinks. Rennie would much have preferred to leave, but there was no option but to sit down with the others.

"I hope you can find time to stay with us for a couple of days, Scott," Dev said hospitably when he had settled down in his chair.

"Thanks very much. I'll admit I was hoping to do just that," said the other man. "Presumptuous of me to turn up out of the blue like this with no warning."

"Not at all," said Dev equably. "That sort of thing happens constantly out here. You can always be sure of hospitality—we like to see visitors from the outside world."

Vince took a long drink from his glass. "Frankly, I'd call *this* the outside world. I'm one of those people who've never seen what some folks call the real Australia—I'm a city person. But when I had young Isobel's last letter, I thought the time had definitely come. I couldn't make up my mind whether she'd fallen in love with this place of yours or whether she couldn't get back to Adelaide fast enough. In any case, there was I, demanding my pound of flesh, the articles she'd promised, in other words. So I thought I'd better come out and find out for myself what it was all about. And maybe help her make up her mind."

Competition for Dev, wondered Rennie. She wondered, too, just what Vince would find out. She didn't think that Isobel had fallen in love with Nimmitibel, but she had certainly fallen in love with Dev. . . .

"Well, you've come in the nick of time," said Dev.

"Another few days and it's my guess you wouldn't have got here."

"No? How's that?"

"We're going to have some rain."

They all looked out a clear cloudless sky, almost dark and pricked with the brightness of of pale large stars.

"I can feel it in the air," said Dev with a faint smile. "And when it comes, the track out from Silver Springs will probably be impassible. You'd have made it so far," he admitted, "but there you'd have come to a full stop."

The expression on Isobel's face was almost comically horrified and even accusing.

Dev leaned forward to refill Vince's glass, glanced at Rennie who had scarcely touched her drink, topped up his own and said with one of his slightly crooked smiles, "Never fear, Isobel. I've got my eye on your interests. I wouldn't allow you to be stranded here."

Isobel looked at Rennie. "Perhaps we shouldn't stay. Perhaps it would be better if Vince took us back to Silver Springs—"

"Oh, come on now," said Vince reasonably. "I've made it all this way—can't we trust in Dev? I want you to show me around. I don't intend going back to civilization without seeing what there is to see." He gave his attention to Dev once more, while Isobel sipped her drink, her eyes downcast, her expression now inscrutable.

So it's to happen at last, thought Rennie. In a very few days she would be leaving Nimmitibel—and Dev—forever. And what of Isobel? Would Dev ask her to come back? Would he promise her Silver Springs? She put that thought quickly aside, thought of Jake instead and wished that they hadn't parted on such unfriendly terms. She would have to try to put that right somehow.

Vince was saying, "By the look of the country, I imagine you could well do with a drop of rain."

"Yes, now is the time for it." Dev produced cigarettes and offered them all around. "It's been a good year for us. We had three inches of rain back in the winter. The feed's been good. If we have a couple of inches spread over the next week or two, and let's say an inch around Christmas time, we'll be all right for summer feed."

Vince laughed. "Hardly sounds adequate to me, but I presume you know what you're talking about. And you claim this rain is on its way now?"

"It is. And we're going to have plenty. That's why I say its fortunate you came when you did."

"Do you mean you expect to be entirely cut off here?"

"Not as bad as that. We can generally get across the track east to Nuripinna station. We have a border muster coming up there tomorrow, as a matter of fact, and should just get it over before the rain comes, with a little luck. . . . And from Nuripinna, we can take the road through the spinifex across the border into New South Wales and then down to Broken Hill. And from there, you can get to wherever you want to."

"Sounds complicated," said Vince. "I think I'd settle for digging myself in here and waiting for it all to be over."

"Which is what we do. But it's good to know that in an emergency we aren't helpless. Unfortunately my airstrip is not an all-weather one—I'll have to remedy that some day but Nuripinna's is."

He smiled at Isobel, who shuddered and said, "You didn't tell me all that before, Dev."

"I didn't think it was the sort of thing you wanted to know," he said lightly. And that, for some reason, brought a very odd expression to Isobel's blue eyes.

Rennie quietly rose to her feet. "If you'll excuse me, I'll go and start dinner. It's getting late."

"Make it a good grilled steak, Rennald," said Dev. "We cattlemen always like to turn out a good steak for city visitors."

DEV DEVOTED HIMSELF to playing the host for the next couple of days. He took Vince and Isobel out to the muster on the Nuripinna station boundary, some fifty miles away. Rennie didn't go. She wanted to see Jake again before she left, but not under those circumstances. She would have to see him privately. Moreover, she didn't care for the idea of making a fourth where three made a complete party—two admiring men and one vivacious and attractive girl who, as long as she could forget the threat of being stranded, was going to enjoy herself very much. So long as the heat didn't overcome her, Rennie reflected, remembering the other muster they had attended.

Her refusal to come displeased Dev.

"What are you going to do with yourself all alone? We'll be gone all day."

"I can entertain myself. I'll write some letters, wash my hair. . . ."

His eyes mocked her. "There'll be no romantic meeting down at the water hole. There's a pretty important muster in progress, remember. Maybe the break will give your ardor a chance to cool down and get you over your infatuation with my head stockman—and don't protest that it's love."

Rennie bit her lip and said nothing. She was not going to give him the satisfaction of knowing that she had broken off her friendship—she had never been infatuated—with Jake already.

When they drove off, she watched from the veranda

with an oddly sore heart, wishing for a moment that she had gone with them after all. But it would simply have made more memories to feed a fire that must be extinguished. It was wise, sensible, not to have gone. And how she hated being wise and sensible!

She washed her hair and wrote to her sister Margo. She talked to Etta and the lubras, to the men in the horseyard. And no matter what she did, she couldn't stop herself from wondering about Isobel Sandison. Had she indirectly invited her boss to come out here? And if so, why? Long ago, Nina had told Rennie that Isobel's boss was in love with her, and it would have been obvious, even if she had never been told. Vince Scott thought Isobel was perfection.

So what game was Isobel playing? Was she in love with two men, trying to make up her mind between them? Or was Dev being difficult was she afraid that if he married her she would have to live at Nimmitibel? In that case, she could be trying to force the issue by arousing his jealousy. . . .

That night after dinner, Vince took Isobel out to walk in the garden. Rennie, who had been carrying the coffee cups out to the kitchen, returned unsuspectingly to find Dev alone.

"The others have gone into the garden. Shall we do likewise, Rennald?" His blue eyes were quizzical, and she had to look away from them. She should have said no but, she argued with herself, what was the alternative? To sit there with him on the veranda, knowing that she would not be able to keep her eyes off him, wondering if he would read what was in them. . . .

She said, with an attempt at casual indifference, "If you like."

"I do like. Do you want a wrap?" He looked at her bare arms. She was wearing a dress tonight, a clinging blue and green affair that made the most of her sea-blue eyes. He took that in, and her tall slender young figure, her long slim-ankled legs, her shining newly-washed hair. And of course the little scar, that he connected with her heart. Then they went down the steps together, and he put his hand lightly on her arm. She felt herself shiver at his touch, although she had shaken her head and refused a wrap.

"We'd better bypass the garden, I think. Isobel and her boss have plenty to talk about," he said. Was there irony in his voice? A trace of bitterness? Or was it as simple as that? Was Isobel talking shop to her boss? "A staid and prosaic walk for us down to the horse paddock and back. Isn't that what you'd like? At least we'll have the moon to admire."

It wasn't, as it happened, a staid and prosaic walk to the stables. Before they had even reached the horse paddock she was in his arms and he was kissing her, and she hadn't the least idea how it had happened. She did know, though, that she was kissing him back and that she could not help herself.

He released her gently at last, but his arms were still loosely around her waist, holding her there a willing but slightly dazed prisoner.

"Rennie."

He said her name, and that was absolutely all. He looked down into her face and his eyes were two blue shadows, his mouth was curving a little and where his hair fell across his forehead it looked smokily black. It was heaven to stand there so close to him, her lips burning from the touch of his, his long fine hands lightly caressing her back, his eyes exploring her face—blue-shadowed and mysterious as his own.

Heaven, but . . . .

She thought of those two others walking in the garden,

in the shadows made by the same moon that gleamed silver gold in a jet black sky and seemed to belong only above Nimmitibel here in the vast Outback. Was it the thought of Isobel possibly in someone else's arms that had made Dev embrace her as he had? And wasn't she a naïve little fool to let it mean anything to her—to be so bemused? She sought for something brittle and sophisticated to say to prove to him that she knew how little it all meant. But quite simply, she couldn't do it. If she had nothing else, she would have this. Why tear the petals off a rose if it is a rose that someone you love has touched?

Perhaps five seconds passed, and then in the silence of the night there was the soft sound of footsteps. Dev dropped his arms, and together they walked out into the moonlight and on toward the horse-paddock rail. They said nothing, but Rennie's heart was beating quickly, and she fancied she could hear its hurried thud as she walked at Dev's side.

The other two caught up with them at the rails.

"A favorite occupation," said Dev, his smile showing white in the moonlight. "Leaning on the rail looking at the horses."

"Hmm—it has a lot to recommend it," agreed Vince. His arm was around Isobel's waist, but Dev and Rennie stood a foot apart. A foot apart, yet possibly, in Vince Scott's mind, romantically linked, if it pleased him to think that way. And Isobel ... what must she think? Rennie felt with sudden weariness that both Dev and Isobel were playing a game of cat and mouse, and she hated herself for helping the game along.

She avoided Dev deliberately the next day and wasn't tempted by his suggestion of a picnic by the water hole later in the afternoon.

He had taken the jeep out before daylight, presumably to the border muster. Rennie woke from a light sleep to hear him go, and he didn't reappear till an hour or two after lunch. Isobel and Vince had amused themselves all morning, and when Dev came in, she heard him suggesting a swim and a picnic.

"Great," enthused Vince, and Isobel said it would be lovely.

Rennie leaned out onto the veranda and said, "I'll pack you a picnic basket," and disappeared.

Dev, who had showered, came into the kitchen ten minutes later. "You're coming, aren't you?" His blue eyes searched her face, pale after a restless night, and she noted absently how dark and thick his lashes were, how they curled up at the tips, and how dark his hair looked when it was damp.

She told him pleasantly, "No, thanks. I'll stay out of it. I wasn't brought here to mix with your guests socially."

"My God, you're an aggravating little girl!" he exclaimed. "You're as variable as water—an Aquarian, I'd guess," he added, and was unexpectedly right. "Well, please yourself, stay home and sulk."

"Sulk?" she repeated.

"Yes, sulk. Isn't it what you've been doing ever since my head stockman was tied up at the border muster? Wasn't that why you received my kisses so prettily last night because you've been missing your little bit of romance?"

Rennie stared at him, her cheeks flaming.

"Come on, let's hear you deny it."

She almost did. But to deny it would be to confess to something else—that she had received Dev's kisses so "prettily" because they were the only kisses she wanted.

She turned away and began slicing cold beef for the picnic basket. She heard herself say, "I didn't know you took the odd kiss so seriously, Mr. Deveraux. I thought you were more sophisticated."

There was a tiny pause. "So I am, *Miss Baxter*," he said through his teeth. "And if we were somewhere else at this moment I'd prove it to you. But not while you have that murderous-looking knife in your hand."

After that, he didn't bother to press her to come to the picnic. And time went by in a sort of nightmare.

THE FOLLOWING DAY even Rennie could feel the change in the atmosphere. The rains were surely coming, and with the disturbance in the air she felt a corresponding disturbance about Jake. She could not leave Nimmitibel with this bitterness between them.

Dev took Isobel and Vince out in the morning, and this time there was no mention of her joining them. She felt ridiculously hurt and ignored, even though she knew she would have refused to go as a matter of principle. She wished she didn't have this hang-up: it was plainly preventing her from getting the most out of her Outback adventure.

After a lunch, during which she ate practically nothing and contributed no more than a polite monosyllable or two to the conversation, she took a brief siesta. Then, instead of joining the others on the veranda, she had Pokataroo saddled up and rode down toward the water hole. The rains would come soon, and then everything would have to be resolved. For herself, it would simply be goodbye. The fact that she would never see Dev again was appalling, yet what troubled her most was, strangely, the thought of Jake, with his stone-hard green eyes, his fantastic good looks and his twisted outlook on life that she had aggravated rather than lessened.

She knew in her heart that she would always long to come back to this country. There was something so savage and primeval yet beautiful about it—a wild, untamed, untamable land. Its colors—the scarlet of the sand, the purple of the shadows, the silver gold of the clumps of coarse grass, the pale limitless dome of the sky—were out of this world. She rode fast across the sandy ground and twice she saw what she had seldom seen—emus running single file along a distant fence. Today the air seemed to lack its usual clarity. The light blue of the sky had a heavier tinge, and there were no water mirages beckoning from the horizon.

But there were birds about in thousands—perching in the trees, screeching and squabbling and starting up into the sky, then settling again. Then, although there was nothing that Rennie could discern to disturb them—not the cracking of a branch, not a sound or a movement but her own horse's quiet progress—it would all begin again.

She looked down toward the water hole in its screen of trees and thought of Jake. But he was fifty miles or more away, out at the border muster. And then her eye was caught by a faint movement. She sprang down from the saddle and moved into the feathery tree shade to watch. It was a whirlwind starting up.

A wisp of sand rose furtively like smoke, fumbling, searching, running delicately out across the bare ground. It snaked this way and that until, with a sudden mad flurry, it began spinning around. In ten seconds it had become a giant, a swirling colossus, a sky-high column of dust and sand and snatched leaves and fragments of grass and scrub and dead branches that careered across the plain in a demented, haphazard dance.

She watched in half-fearful fascination, sure that this giddy, staggering monster was alive and aware of her—sure that at any moment she herself would be caught up, engulfed, fragmented. Yet unable to tear herself away from it, she watched until, suddenly, it collapsed and disappeared as if by witchcraft.

And instead of the whirlwind, Dev stood there, seemingly conjured up out of nothingness. Rennie stared for a moment, sure that he was not real, that he, too, was some kind of genie, and then without thinking she ran to meet him, throwing herself into his arms. They were real enough, and she was caught up in the whirlwind of his eyes, her senses were spinning. He held her and kissed her crazily. It was as if she were at the very heart of the whirlwind, at its very center, helpless, lost, entirely possessed. . . .

His head slackened for an instant and it was then that she heard someone whistling and recognized that tune of Jake's, "The Dying Stockman." And over Dev's shoulders in the still waters of the pool, where the strange clouded blue of the sky lay heavy and thick and solid as a sheet of glass, she saw a reflection move.

Jake!

Without knowing it, she drew back from Dev. Her eyes were raised to the red sandy bank above the water where Jake stood, smiling across at her, a little beseechingly, a little bitterly.

"Jake!" His name floated from her lips on a breath, and she felt herself shaken by a strange shuddering spasm.

The man whose arms were still around her turned his head.

"Jake?" His voice was harsh, discordant, so that the name sounded ugly.

But now there was no one there—nothing not a movement among the trees. Not a shadow on the water, not a ripple. Stupefied, shaking, Rennie looked at Dev, and his eyes were hard, their pupils like pinpoints.

"Afraid Jake Ridley might catch you kissing me? You don't need to worry. He's fifty miles away, working to get that muster through before the rain comes." He had released her now and was looking down at her with cold distant eyes that scarcely seemed to see her as another human being. "That's why I'm here. I came to find you and ask you " he stopped abruptly and rephrased it "– to tell you to get back to the homestead and pack up and be on your way. You can have a lift with Vince Scott."

CHAPTER NINE

RENNIE'S HEAD WAS BOWED as if she had received execution orders. But still she was haunted by the image of the man she had seen, looking at her across the calm water. Reality or ghost? And if the latter, then what was Jake Ridley's ghost doing here, looking so beseechingly at her?

She glanced back at the water hole before she got back into the saddle to ride with Dev back to Nimmitibel. For the last time.

They rode side by side in an inimical, distant, unbreakable silence. There were miles between them spiritually, and it would always be so. Rennie's heart ached.

Back at the homestead, Isobel was getting Vince to load her gear into his car as fast as ever it could be managed.

"Go in and pack," Dev told Rennie quietly.

To that Isobel added a near-hysterical, "And for goodness' sake hurry! We don't want to be stuck out here for weeks."

In her bedroom, Rennie mindlessly and stupidly bundled her clothes from drawers and wardrobe into her suitcases without bothering to fold them. It was all ending too soon for her to cope with it. She thrust her toilet things into her zipper bag, closed it up and caught a glimpse of herself in the mirror. Her hair was loose, her face pale, her scar blazing as she had never seen it blaze before. She was still wearing jeans and shirt, but no matter. She took a suitcase in each hand, and with the soft travel case tucked under one arm, staggered into the hall and across the veranda. As she went, she heard the telephone shrilling in the office. She heard Dev swearing, and then he brushed past her and went in to answer it.

Isobel was now sitting in the car waiting and Vince, smoking a cigarette, stood nearby.

"Hurry up," snapped Isobel. "We've been waiting for you for ages."

The sky had turned a strange dusty pinkish gray and everything was deathly still. Somewhere a long way off a cockatoo screeched, and in the paddock a horse whinnied. Vince took Rennie's luggage and stowed it in the trunk of the car, saw her into the back seat and closed the door.

"Where's Dev?" asked Isobel petulantly.

"He's on the telephone," said Rennie coldly.

"For heaven's sake—just when we're trying to get away? Who's he calling?"

"No one. Someone's calling him."

"Then I wish they'd save their social calls for some other time. If he doesn't come out soon, we might as well go. He knows perfectly well we must hurry. If the rain starts now we could be stuck here for ever, and I'll be totally . . . totally manic."

Her voice broke, and Vince said placatingly, "There now, don't get temperamental, darling. It won't happen as suddenly as that."

"In this country? It could do anything," wailed Isobel, who was clearly on the point of breaking down and crying.

Vince lit a cigarette and handed it to her. "See if that will soothe your nerves. You've put yourself through too much this time, darling, and if I'd known it was a sort of minor Hades out here I'd have come and collected you long ago. Now calm down! Dev will be out soon, we'll say goodbye and thank you and in next to no time it will all be over. You'll have forgotten all the bad things and you'll only remember the fun you had.''

"And won't I be glad,'' said Isobel, puffing nervously on her cigarette, her hand shaking. "I've never been so homesick for the city! I thought I could take it, and then when you came, Vince, I saw it all for what it is.'' She shuddered. "An all-but-derelict old homestead, and this ghastly burning desert all around.''

A low rumble of thunder sounded, and the sky, which had been darkening perceptibly, was now full of racing clouds, though there still seemed to be not a breath of air down on the plain. A few drops of rain fell and Rennie felt a strange stirring in her heart. Dev's rain, the rain that was needed, the rain that would make green things grow and insure the cattle of their summer feed. But she would not be here to see it all happen.

At that moment, Dev came down from the veranda. His face was strained, its muscles taut. He came to the car and opened Rennie's door.

"Get your things out, Rennald. I've got to get you to the Nuripinna border.''

"Why?'' She felt her hear contract with fear. Her cheeks whitened and her eyes were fixed on his face a deadly serious face. Isobel and Vince were silent, staring at him uncomprehendingly.

"I'll explain in a minute,'' he said briefly. She climbed out of the car like one in a dream and watched dazedly while he and Vince hauled her stuff out of the trunk and set it on the ground. He had said something in a low voice to the other man, but Rennie did not hear what it was. She only knew that Vince looked concerned.

The two men shook hands. She heard Dev say goodbye

to Isobel, saw him lean down and kiss her through the car window. The next minute Vince had driven off and she and Dev were alone.

"What's happened?" she heard herself ask. Somewhere inside she knew. It was Jake. . . .

, "That was a call from Nuripinna station," he told her, and suddenly his voice was gentle. "There's been an accident at the muster. Jake Ridley took a fall from his horse." He stopped and his eyes searched her face. "They've sent to Broken Hill for the flying doctor. It's . . . bad." She saw a grave compassion in his blue eyes. "I'm sorry about this, Rennie. He's asked for you."

She nodded slowly, her face deathly white. "You mean he's " Dying, but she did not say it.

"Yes." His expression was abstracted, almost hard. "It was going to happen sooner or later—I've known it for a long time. We get a man like Jake on the property now and again, a man who's ceased to value his life and who's careless to the point of recklessness with it. It always ends the same way. There's an accident." As he spoke they had been walking toward the garages, and now he was helping her into the jeep. "I'm just sorry that it should end this way for you—with such cruel and pointless drama. I suppose it's no use asking you not to take it too hard—a love affair is a love affair." His eyes were troubled and he hesitated before he got in beside her. "Perhaps you'd rather not go out there."

Rennie was struggling to keep back tears. Now was not the time to deny a love affair—he had called it infatuation before—and certainly she was not going to refuse to go to a dying man whom once she had thought of, perhaps foolishly, as a friend. She said, her throat constricted, "I must go." She knew that she must see him, smile for him, touch his hand. She remembered how he had said he loved her, and how she had tossed the words disbeliev-

ingly back at him, even while she had realized he spoke
as if he meant it. She had not been strong enough to help
him and she had parted from him without even taking
his hand. How much of the fault in their ill-fated relationship had lain with her? She didn't understand men
like Jake Ridley, she lacked the experience in life. She
should have kept away from him from the start as Dev
had warned her to do. But she had been careless, way-
ward, overconfident. And now. . . . She bit hard on her
lip to keep back tears.

As they drove out to the airstrip big drops of rain fell
intermittently, sending the red dust up in tiny wraiths,
leaving an infinitesimal trail of steam. And the whole
world—the sky and the earth, even the trees themselves—
was a weird and dusty pink.

Dev said, "If there was time, we could drive out to the
camp. But we must get there the fastest way we can—and
even so, we might not be in time. I'll have to put down on
the Nuripinna airstrip for safety's sake, and from there
someone will run us over to the muster camp."

They had reached the hangar, and now she was
hurrying after Dev. She said, without even being aware
that she had entertained the thought, "Couldn't
you . . . couldn't you drop me down, Dev? It would be
the quickest way, and—" She stopped, unable to go on,
letting her eyes tell Dev how important it was that she
should get there in time.

He hesitated and she was aware of his strong reluctance. He said with a heavy sigh, "It's going to be a hard
experience for you, Rennie. Not one that I'd have chosen
for you to have in any case. Such drama can make it hard
to forget, to recover. . . . But there's no point in you
taking risks with your life."

She interrupted him passionately, "I *must* get to him—
I must. Nothing will go wrong. There'll be no risk at all."

"I told you long ago you were never to touch my gear again," he said savagely. Then suddenly, unexpectedly, he added, "All right—if it must be so."

Seconds later she was getting into the parachuting gear, and Dev was fastening the straps that her shaking hands couldn't manage.

By the time they were airborne, the sky had cleared miraculously and the big drops of rain were no longer falling. A blaze of sunlight fell across the red earth below, and Rennie thanked heaven. She could not have parachuted down if the rain had thickened.

They flew out over the Nimmitibel runway, over the red plain with its long, flat-topped ridges, its clumps of mulga and its tiny silvery water holes. And then away below she could see the tiny figures of stockmen on horseback, and two great mobs of cattle, one herd coming in toward Nimmitibel, the other going slowly toward a dam on Nuripinna. There was no fence at all to show where one property ended and the other began.

Dev drew her attention to a thick drift of smoke coming from the darkness of trees.

"There's the camp—and your wind direction. Your dropping zone will be down there on that open patch of ground. Do you think you can manage it?"

She nodded. "Easily."

"Don't be too sure. Take care. I'll tell you when to jump."

"What will you do, Dev? Will you come in from Nuripinna?"

He shrugged. "I'll join you as soon as I can. I might manage to find myself a landing strip a little closer in."

"Don't take any chances," she said quickly, and saw his mouth twist.

"Look who's talking!" Then half below his breath he added, "You're a girl with a great heart. It's a pity we . . . well, I'll see you later. Don't waste time packing up the chute: leave it on the ground. Now are you ready?"

He banked, came in over the trees, the engine cut out and he shouted "Go!" In a split second the whole of her life seemed to pass before her eyes and then she was into the slipstream and on her own.

It was the neatest, quietest descent she had ever made in her life, and in her heart she felt that she had made her last jump. She would never want to parachute down through the sky again.

She collapsed the canopy and shed her gear as fast as she could, though her hands were shaking again. A stockman had come from among the trees ahead to meet her.

"In here," he told her briefly.

She looked quickly up at the sky. A few clouds had moved over again, and she could hear the engine of the Cessna. It sounded as if Dev were flying very low, or even coming down.

"The Cessna?" she asked as she hurried along beside the bleak-eyed, silent stockman.

"The boss will put it down this end of the wilga paddock he's done it before. My cobber's taken one of the horses across to meet him. He'll be all right, miss. Don't you worry."

Jake lay on the ground on a bedding roll, his body covered by a checked blanket. His face looked cold, his black hair was tumbled, and for a long moment Rennie could only stand silently, her heart in her mouth, terribly afraid and wondering if she was too late. Then she moved quietly forward and dropped to her knees on the ground beside him.

"Jake," she whispered.

His eyes opened, their strange yellow green color like a

flame, a light a light that flickered over her face with a heart-stirring hunger. His lips moved and he managed a twisted smile.

"I knew you'd fly to me, Renniebird. I knew we hadn't reached the end of the story." His voice was a mere whisper, and she had to bend her head to hear it. One hand moved to free itself from the blanket, and she put her own over its coldness.

He closed his eyes and a long time went by. She sat with Jake's hand in her own, and it seemed strange that they could be together like this—that the passion, the desire that had flared in him too strongly should have died away, been subdued. And yet she had a curious feeling that he was satisfied.

The stockman who had come to find her coughed a little and she looked up. His eyes were black, his lips somber, a thin tight line. He offered her cigarettes, and she shook her head. He began to talk, squatting on his haunches, his back against a tree.

"Beats me how a man like Jake got thrown—an ace rider, one in a million. But it happens. Could have been any one of us. I've never yet worked on a ranch where a stockman hasn't been killed some time or another." He stopped abruptly and looked up at the sky. "Rain's holding off, giving the flying doctor a chance to get through. It'll come down soon enough."

Silence fell between them again, and presently Jake's hand moved a little under Rennie's. His eyes opened the merest slit.

"You were right, Renniebird," he whispered. "You wouldn't have been . . . the girl I loved if you'd . . . given in to me. For that I . . . thank you. . . . Believe me?" His eyes watched her, but this time they remained unmovingly on her own eyes, and she nodded.

"Yes, I believe you, Jake—of course."

"Kiss me. There's a sweet girl."

She leaned forward and kissed him, touched his tumbled hair and felt hot tears slide down her cheeks.

"I . . . love you," he said. It was all he could manage, but his eyes were open fully for a second, yellow green and clear as spring leaves and showing plainly what he had admitted to—love. A smile lifted the corners of his mouth, but his lean cheeks were suddenly pallid beneath their leathery suntan. His fingers tightened on her own and then his lids came down.

Someone moved behind her and she looked around to see Dev standing there. She stumbled to her feet and now it was he who knelt beside Jake. She turned her back to wipe away tears. Dimly she was aware of a plane droning through the sky, but she knew that nothing could help Jake now. He was close to the end of everything this world held for him.

He didn't open his eyes again. Dev and the other stockman smoked and talked occasionally in low voices, and Dev glanced across at Rennie once or twice, his blue eyes grave, watchful.

Then at last there was the sound of a motor, and in a minute the flying doctor was there.

Rennie went away, out of the trees and across to the place on the bare red earth where she had left the chute. Methodically and mindlessly, her eyes dry, she began to field-pack it.

She was just finishing when Dev came. He stood, hands on his hips, looking down at her. His eyes were no longer blue, but black and bleak and empty.

"I thought it best for you not to go. He has family in Broken Hill—two brothers, a sister and a—"

"A wife," she said, her voice low. She stood up and looked across at him and she was shivering. Without knowing it, she took one small tentative step toward him as if seeking comfort.

The next second, he had covered the space between them, and she was in his arms, held closely, his face against her hair.

"For God's sake," he muttered, his voice husky, "don't look at me with such great tragic eyes. How can I help you? Is it any use to say that he was a deeply unhappy man until you did something to his heart? But, God knows it could never have worked out—believe me, Rennie. You're young and perhaps you think it could have, but his bitterness, his grudge against life, against women, went too deep for him ever to get over."

She had begun to weep a little. She thought of those hard eyes, and she knew that it was true. It was only when death was near that Jake could soften and admit love. In life he had been too ready to believe himself despised. At the last, he knew he had asked too much. But Dev was wrong if he imagined she had ever envisaged a permanent relationship with Jake. She moved a little from him, and looked up at him through lashes that were wet with her tears.

"I was never in love with him," she said shakily. "I tried to be . . . his friend. We . . . quarreled over that. I was never going to see him again. That was why it was so important for me to come. He . . . forgave me at the last for not being more. Thank you for making it easy—"

"Easy?" he asked. He looked down at her and his lips moved, but he could say no more.

It had started to rain—a fine, steady rain—and suddenly they were both aware of it.

She said, "What are you going to do with me now?"

He didn't answer. He lifted the parachute pack from red earth that the rain was staining quickly to brilliance and put his arm across her shoulders. It was a rough comfort such as she had never known, and she felt her tears begin again. They walked back in silence to what was left of the camp under the trees, where two stockmen were packing up the bedding roll, the checked blanket, the odds and ends of paraphernalia that had lain about.

Dev said, his voice sounding odd, not like his usual voice at all, not firm and commanding and sure of itself, "I need a couple of horses to get this girl and myself out to the Cessna. Andy?"

"Right, boss." The stockman who had brought Rennie to Jake gave him a too-bright grin. "I'll be the escort."

They jogged through drizzle across the red plain and through more trees to the wilga paddock where the plane waited.

"Will you get her off the ground all right?" Andy asked.

Dev looked at his Cessna, then at Rennie. "This girl's a mere featherweight. But I'll leave the gear," he decided.

The parachuting gear was dumped on the ground, and Rennie and Dev got into the Cessna. It was not an easy takeoff, but it was accomplished. From the air, Rennie looked down and saw a stockman leading two horses back to join his mate. One of the horses was loaded with the parachute pack.

She drew a sigh that seemed to come from the depths of her heart. It was goodbye to a lot of things today. . . .

That night she slept in the Nimmitibel homestead, and for propriety's sake old Etta slept in one of the other bedrooms—the one where, until tonight, Isobel had slept. Rennie's was a long, exhausted, dreamless sleep, and when she woke late in the morning it was because the old aboriginal woman had brought her a cup of tea—black, strong and very sweet. A little of it had slopped over into the saucer, soaking into the thick slice of buttered bread that lay alongside.

"This do you good, Rennie," Etta said. "You sleep good?"

"Very good, thank you."

She could hear the soft sound of rain on the iron roof as she sat on the edge of the bed drinking her tea. It seemed strange that there was no hot sunshine reflected in from the garden across the veranda.

Presently she showered in the big black and white tiled bathroom. She wondered where Dev was. The homestead seemed strangely empty, but when she had dressed and gone through to the veranda, she saw that outside it was busy. The stockmen were in from the muster because there would be no more work with the cattle until the rain was over. She could see them down at their quarters beyond the garden, engaged in various activities, or simply sitting smoking and exchanging stories. Jake should have been there, she thought, and her heart ached.

Later the telephone rang, and as there seemed to be no one else around, Rennie answered it. She wondered if it would be Isobel, wanting Dev. But it was Dr. Grace, her voice sharp.

"Is that you, Rennald? I was hoping Dev would have taken you to Nuripinna. We heard the news this morning about his head stockman. These accidents always happen—they can be very upsetting. I can't think why you had to be dragged into it. Isobel says there was something between you and Jake Ridley, but of course that's all a lot of nonsense. . . . Is Dev around?"

"I'll see if I can find him," said Rennie, a sudden lump in her throat.

"Oh, don't bother. It was mostly on your account I

rang. I wish you had come across with Isobel and her friend yesterday. I wonder if there's any chance of your coming over?''

"I'll ask Dev is he thinks the track's passable," said Rennie.

A hand reached across her shoulder and took the telephone from her.

"Hello? What's happening there, Grace? Isobel—"

Rennie had to stay where she was because Dev's arm was around her. She couldn't hear what Grace was saying at the other end of the line and she wondered what Isobel and Vince Scott were doing, and what Dev felt about it all. Then he said, "Fine, fine—I'm glad to hear it. And what about you?" Grace talked again, and Dev's hand moved gently on Rennie's shoulder. "I think you're wise. Yes, he's an extremely likable young fellow—very competent. I'm pleased you've changed your mind. As you say, we'll see. . . . I think it's most unlikely that I can drive over that track and then get back again. Don't worry, I'll work out something. . . . Just don't feel responsible, Grace. Leave it all to me. Yes, of course I'll let you know. . . . Yes, it was a bad thing. . . . Thank you."

When he had hung up, he gave Rennie a long and searching scrutiny.

"Did you sleep well? You're not looking as weary and shaken up as you did last night. Has Etta been taking care of you?"

"Yes, thank you. I'm sorry to be causing you all this trouble."

"Trouble?" he repeated absently. She wondered what he was thinking about. His blue eyes gave the impression that he was intent on some inner problem.

She asked, because she had to, "What is Isobel going to do?"

He looked at her in surprise. "Isobel? Oh, Isobel and Scott and poor long-suffering Miss Sandison left for Adelaide early this morning. I think they'd all seen as much as they wanted of the Outback."

"Isobel would have stayed at Silver Springs," said Rennie. There was a bowl of roses on the desk. Was it only yesterday that she had cut and arranged them and put them there for Dev? She pulled one of them free, a lovely cream and gold rose, and laid it against her cheek where she could catch its fragrance.

"What do you mean by that?" He sat on the corner of the desk and his eyes wouldn't leave her alone.

She looked at him over the golden petals. "You said that for the girl you loved you'd leave Nimmitibel."

He watched her steadily. Then he reached across and took the rose from her. "Do you want me to leave Nimmitibel, Rennie?" he asked quietly.

She felt a shock in her heart, then tears flew to her eyes. She stared at him, unable to understand—to believe.

"You're the girl I love," he said.

"Not Isobel?" she said stupidly. "But—but you invited her here . . . to see how she like it . . . to—"

His eyebrows peaked quizzically. "I invited her because it would have been churlish not to. She confided in me that she wanted to write some articles about my part of the country."

"But she—" Rennie stopped.

"She lost her head a little over me," he agreed carelessly. "I knew that a good strong dose of the Outback would soon get her over that and send her back to her home paddock. As it did. I'll admit I found her attractive enough. I'm a male animal, Rennie, and I've never lived the life of a monk. Women have been important to me. But none of them—until you came—was as important as Nimmitibel."

"Me?" she whispered, her eyes on his.

His answer was to pull her to him and prove it with his arms around her and his mouth against hers.

Several minutes later they left the office and went through to the veranda to watch the rain falling on the plain and sharpening the colors to brightness under a strange gray sky.

"Tell me," said Rennie simply, as they stood at the railing, his arm across her shoulders.

He said, "I love you. And for me that's the beginning and the end. And you?"

"I love you, too, Dev," she said unsteadily.

"And are you going to tell me about the love affair or whatever it was that left you with that scar on your cheek and a suspicion of men?"

"It was nothing," said Rennie, and meant it. "Just my jump instructor who turned out to have a fiancée already."

"The girl in the sky who upset your equilibrium? And that's all over?"

"Long ago."

"I couldn't understand. You were a girl who had to be handled with kid gloves. You were so determined when we first met to let me know that men were the least of your interests out here—"

She smiled a little. "I was still getting over Pete then. But most of my fervor on that occasion was on Nancy's account. I . . . I thought you were Jake . . . and—" Her voice faltered and she broke off and felt his fingers tighten on her shoulder.

"You can tell me later about that, Rennie." There was a moment's silence. "You know," he said then, "you intrigued me very much that day with your positive assertion that you were the cook, and that you'd come to see the country, not the male population. And those

daredevil eyes of yours! Yet when I invited you to
Nimmitibel, because I knew I had to find out more about
you—you just weren't interested. And I wondered if all
that fire was simply running through dry grass and had
burned itself out in a minute.''

"I wouldn't come because of Isobel," she admitted. "I
didn't want to be . . . played with.''

"So it seemed! But when I made one more effort to
entice you out to Nimmitibel, you took up my challenge
with a vengeance and arrived by parachute. I was sick at
the thought that you might have killed yourself, and I'd
have been responsible because I'd dared you in an
insidious kind of way.'' His eyes grew grave. "I felt even
more responsible when it seemed you'd fallen in love
with Jake. It was an impossible attraction. I hoped it was
mere infatuation, something time would cure, but I never
would have wished you to be put through such a traumatic experience as yesterday. With a young girl like
you, that could have disastrous psychological con-
sequences.''

She shook her head. "I liked him and I tried to
help. . . .''

They looked at each other for an intensely serious
instant.

'There's one other thing,'' he said then. "Grace wants
to stay on at Silver Springs to see if Tim and Nancy are
really serious about each other. As a matter of fact, I
think she hopes they are. She's given me up as a bad
apple and she can picture herself having a free hand at
Silver Springs if Nancy marries the manager and it's
once more the family home. I suspect she'll end up with a
wholesome respect for Tim Lang, however. He's not a
man to let himself be pushed around. . . . But all this
brings me back to the point of what I was going to say.
You're out of a job as from now, Rennie. Grace has

decided to dispense with your services. So what am I going to do with you?"

Rennie looked back at him.

"Marry me," she said simply. They both laughed and she was back in his arms and the tears hung on her lashes again.

"There couldn't be a better solution," he said. "Well, it's a rainy day, there's no work to be done. We can devote ourselves to working out a plan for our future. Agreed?"

"Agreed," she said. And added softly, "Dev."

Remember when a good love story made you feel like holding hands?

The wonder of love is timeless. Once discovered, love remains, despite the passage of time. Harlequin brings you stories of true love, about women the world over – women like you.

Harlequin Romances with the Harlequin magic...

Recapture the sparkle of first love...relive the joy of true romance...enjoy these stories of love today.

Eight new novels every month – wherever paperbacks are sold.